Editor: Talia Leduc

ISBN-13: 978-1998775477

Give feedback on the book at:
lorhainneeckhart@hotmail.com

Twitter: @LEckhart
Facebook: AuthorLorhainneEckhart

Printed in the U.S.A

A Different Kind of Love

THE FRIESSEN LEGACY

THE FRIESSENS: A NEW BEGINNING
BOOK THREE

LORHAINNE ECKHART

The Friessen Family Series
Reading order:

The Outsider Series

The Forgotten Child
A Baby And A Wedding
Fallen Hero
The Awakening
Secrets
Runaway
Overdue
The Unexpected Storm
The Wedding

The Friessens: A New Beginning

The Deadline
The Price to Love
A Different Kind of Love
A Vow of Love, A Friessen Family Christmas

The Friessens

The Reunion
The Bloodline
The Promise
The Business Plan
The Decision
First Love
Family First
Leave the Light On
In the Moment
In the Family: A Friessen Family Christmas
In the Silence
In the Stars
In the Charm
Unexpected Consequences
It Was Always You
The First Time I Saw You
Welcome to My Arms
Welcome to Boston (A Paige & Morgan Short Story)
I'll Always Love You
Ground Rules
A Reason to Breathe
You Are My Everything
Anything For You
The Homecoming includes When They Were Young
Stay Away From My Daughter
The Bad Boy
A Place of Our Own
The Visitor
All About Devon
Long Past Dawn
How to Heal a Heart
Keep Me In Your Heart

The Friessen Family

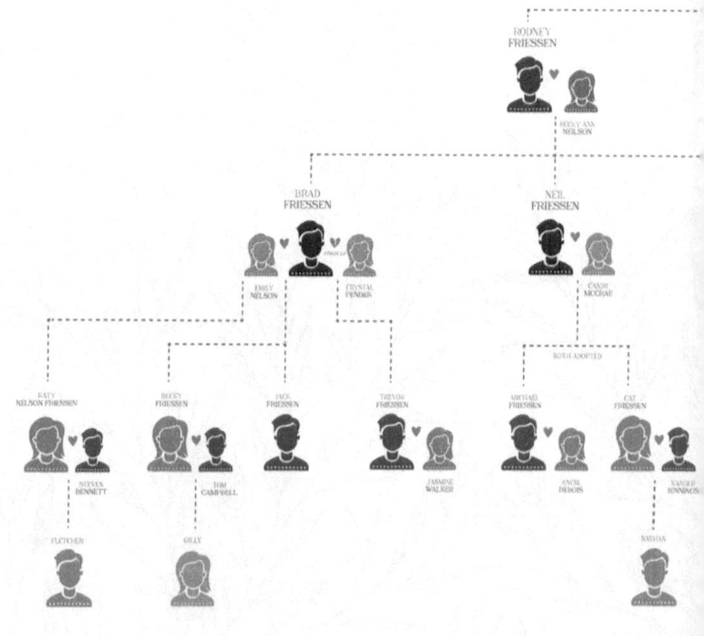

The Outsider Series

THE FORGOTTEN CHILD	BRAD & EMILY
A BABY AND A WEDDING	BRAD & EMILY & *2nd set Sydney & Emily*
FALLEN HERO	JED, DIANA & ANDY
THE SEARCH	JED, DIANA & ANDY
THE AWAKENING	ANDY & LAURA

The Outsider Series

SECRETS	DIANA & JED *with the entire Friessen Family*
RUNAWAY	ANDY & LAURA
OVERDUE	JED & DIANA
THE UNEXPECTED STORM	NEIL & CANDY
THE WEDDING	NEIL & CANDY *and the entire Friessen Family*

The Friessens: A New Beginning

THE DEADLINE	ANDY & LAURA
THE PRICE TO LOVE	NEIL & CANDY
A DIFFERENT KIND OF LOVE	BRAD & EMILY
A VOW OF LOVE	THE ENTIRE
A FRIESSEN FAMILY CHRISTMAS	FRIESSEN FAMILY

The Friessens

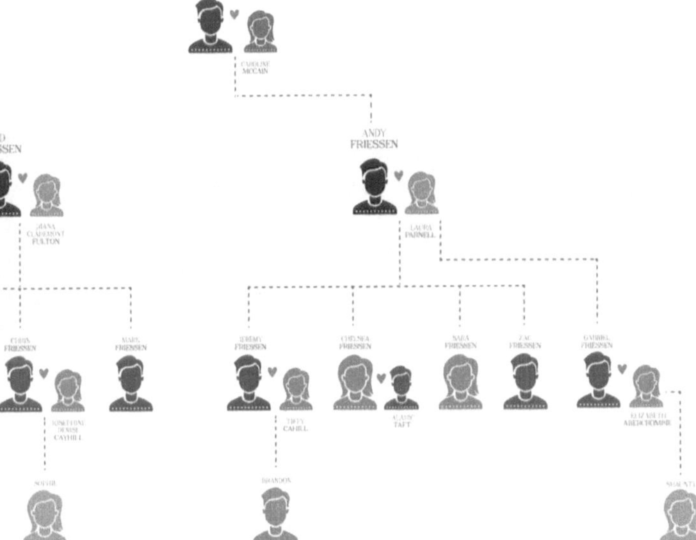

TODD FRIESSEN
CAROLINE McCAIN
ED FRIESSEN
DIANA CLAREMONT FULTON
ANDY FRIESSEN
LAURA PARNELL
CHRIS FRIESSEN
MARY FRIESSEN
JEREMY FRIESSEN
CHELSEA FRIESSEN
SARA FRIESSEN
ZAC FRIESSEN
GABRIEL FRIESSEN
JOSEPHINE DENISE CAYHILL
TIFFY CAHILL
ALARIC TAFT
ELIZABETH ABERCROMBIE
SOPHIE
BRANDON
SHANTI

A Different Kind of Love brings back the couple that started it all: Brad and Emily. You fell in love with them in *The Forgotten Child*. Now, years later, they face an entirely new set of challenges with their preteen autistic boy when his mother, Crystal, returns. She wants a relationship with the boy she abandoned—something Brad and Emily never expected.

She says she's changed, but can the Friessens believe her?

Chapter 1

S he swore it had happened overnight, a shift from hot days and comfortable mornings to a noticeable chill in the air. It was earlier than usual, this very distinct change in seasons from summer to fall. Emily preferred easing in gently, being given time to adjust, over always feeling as if she was on a roller coaster ride and couldn't get off. But this was her life, and if given a choice between this one or one completely different and easy—well, she wouldn't change it for anything. She was human, though, and there were days she wished for nothing but peace.

She could hear the creak of floorboards upstairs where she'd left her husband, Brad, sleeping. He would be wondering where she was when he reached for her. That was just the way it was between them in the mornings, even though they slept curled against one another, his legs entwined and twisted with hers. There wasn't a part of him she didn't love to touch and feel against her. He was the first man to truly have her heart.

He loved her, she loved him, and their children meant

everything to them. This was her family, and it was good—better than good. It was amazing. She loved them all: their little girl Becky, the one child Brad and she shared together, and Katy and Trevor, who were their children from their first marriages. Now she was Trevor's mother, and Brad was Katy's father.

He was on the stairs now. "Em?"

She still loved the sound of his voice; after all these years, he still had the ability to turn her insides to putty. It was so deep and masculine and sexy that she had to fight the urge to run to him, which was something people might call her crazy for if she ever admitted it.

He pushed open the screen door, and she took in his frown from where she leaned against the pillar, bathed in streaks of pink and yellow from the rising sun. "Why didn't you answer me?" He slid his arms around her from behind, pulling her to him, running his flattened palm over the cotton of her nightgown, rubbing against her stomach.

She leaned back into him. He was so warm, and she couldn't imagine ever tiring of the way he held her and how she fit so easily against him. The strength in his arms … she loved running her hands over them, feeling the contrast of the muscle and soft skin and dark hair. He made her feel so secure, as if nothing bad could ever touch her. She sighed in his embrace. He had pulled on a light blue shirt, and its freshly laundered scent mixed with his warmth soothed and stirred her at the same time.

He swayed with her, holding her. She could feel the cut of his biceps, triceps, and pecs, his solid abs pressed against her back. She pictured the feel of them as if they were burned into her memory. She loved to run her hands over all that hardness. She barely passed his shoulders, and he leaned his chin against the top of her head. They rocked together.

"What's wrong?" He pressed a kiss to her forehead, and she breathed him in again. His scent always grounded her.

"I don't know," she replied—and she really didn't. She had woken early and hadn't been able to go back to sleep. An odd stirring feeling had unsettled her. She could feel Brad try to pull back, so she held more tightly to his arm. "No, just hold me like this."

"Are you not feeling well?" He wasn't going to let it go, but then, Brad wasn't a man to just ignore things, not with his family and never with her.

Any fights they had stemmed from him not letting things go. He pushed at times, never letting her hold on to things and sulk. Not that she did. He prodded, always knowing when something was bothering her. They were so in tune with each other. He had such a need to protect her and their children, to the point that she sometimes worried about what would happen if she ever had to stand on her own two feet.

"I couldn't sleep," she said. "Maybe I'm just over-thinking things, with school coming up. I'm just ..." She couldn't figure out how to put into words this unsettling feeling that kept coming at her over and over. Something wasn't right, but she couldn't put her finger on it or explain it to Brad in a sane way.

"You're doing too much again," he said. "I told you to stop planning everything. The kids are back in school. Just let them go." He always made it sound so easy—typical man, thinking everything that worked out wasn't the result of some hardworking woman behind the scenes, planning, organizing, and doing.

"Our little girl is going into first grade, and she's going to be gone all day." Emily's throat thickened.

He didn't laugh at her, and she was so grateful for that.

Maybe he understood. "We could have another baby if you want, and then you'd have your hands full again."

It wasn't as if she hadn't thought about it. "I don't know, Brad. Do you want another?" They hadn't tried to have another baby after Becky was born, and she had been completely unplanned. It wasn't that they were being careful or anything now—just that it hadn't happened since.

"You know I would love a houseful, but you're their mother, and most of the work falls to you, honey."

She knew he loved children and he was their protector, but he had a ranch to run, too. She didn't know if she wanted to start over again with diapers and toddlers and not a moment to herself. Although she wouldn't trade one moment of the time she had with her children, she also realized she had more freedom now, and she didn't want to give it up. "Katy is in gymnastics twice a week now, and Trevor … we need to meet with the school again. His consultant is coming out next week to meet with his teacher to get everything started for the new year. There's just so much to do, Brad."

"Hey, Trevor is fine. You see how far he's come, Em. School's going good. Don't start finding things to worry about. You have everyone so organized that nothing can go wrong," he said. At times, she thought, he didn't worry enough.

"Brad, every year we've had something with the school … some problem, some new teacher who wants to change how we do things, and I have to start at the beginning. Remember two years ago when we had that new teacher who refused to work with our consultant or to make any changes in her teaching methodology to accommodate Trevor? She refused every one of the suggestions we made. I thought you were going to lose it," she said.

She could feel him tense behind her. Sitting with Brad in that meeting room at the school, that had been the first time Emily ever thought he could come unglued. She'd made an excuse to get him out of there: "Don't you have a golf game you're going to be late for?" He didn't golf, of course, but he was sharp enough to pick up on her meaning, and he had nodded and left. When she got home, she had barely walked through the door before he gave her an earful, cursing that teacher with every imaginable fate as he paced the kitchen like a wild beast. He'd calmed down eventually, four hours later. Then the principal had phoned, apologizing profusely and assuring them he'd find a way to make it work. He had, but only when he was teaching. It had been a lost year, and without the education assistant who worked with him in the classroom, Trevor would have learned nothing.

"You don't know that, Em. Besides, we already met the teacher, and you said you liked her."

She could feel her heart tightening. She knew it was just her anxiety working overtime, but maybe he could feel it too, as he kissed her ear and slid his hand up and over her heart, her breast, pressing her closer to him. "I know," she replied. "And I'm sure I'm just expecting the worst, all these back-to-school anxieties. It's just that Trevor has come so far. He's independent in so many things; I don't want someone coming in and screwing it up."

He actually chuckled in her ear, and this time she slid around, taking in the humor in his amazing whiskey-colored eyes. They reached inside her, and they had a connection so deep that she couldn't hide anything from him, even if she wanted to. He had this way of making her feel … better.

"Why are you laughing at me?" she said.

"Em, our kids are so lucky to have you for a mother,

and God help any person who tries to come in and mess with them." He slid his hand over her cheek, pressing in, and his fingers brushed her ear. She couldn't help leaning in closer. He kissed her, holding her other cheek, pulling her to him as he deepened the kiss, which brought that stirring deep inside her that happened every time he touched her. She needed to connect with him, skin to skin, and only he could satisfy her.

"Why don't we go upstairs for that good-morning wakeup you denied me?"

He kissed her again and started leading her into the house, but she pulled back and whispered, "Don't you have cows to feed?"

"They'll wait," he said, and he had her halfway to the stairs when they heard the first sounds of little feet jumping out of bed.

"Yeah, but the kids won't," she said with a groan, leaning into him.

He patted her bottom and then tilted her chin so she was forced to look at him. "I may have to tie you to the bed just to make sure you're there in the morning."

She rolled her eyes. "As if you'd ever do that."

"Hey, if I wake up and my wife isn't in bed with me again—I may consider it!" he said, and he kissed her just as she heard the pitter-patter of their three kids hitting the stairs.

Chapter 2

"See you later, Dad." Trevor had finished packing his backpack and was now zipping it up as Emily raced around the house after the girls. She was fast on Katy and Becky's heels, calling out first for them to get dressed, then to brush their hair and teeth. Then Becky couldn't find her hairbrush, and Katy's pink shoes—which she had to wear, or her first day back would be a disaster—disappeared. Emily still had to get them to organize their supplies and help them pack their lunches. With Trevor, it was easier now that he understood his routine, which, as of late, he had been picking up faster.

"Katy, if you're planning on going to gymnastics after school, I suggest you pack up your body suit. Don't forget a ponytail tie for your hair, either, and a water bottle." Emily snapped her fingers as if just remembering something, or maybe she was sifting through a mental list in her head. "I'm not running to the school because you forgot something!" she called out as she zipped up Katy and Becky's lunch kits after finally packing their lunches herself.

"I know, Mom," Katy yelled from upstairs.

"You got everything you need for school packed?" Brad strode over to Trevor, who was standing beside the kitchen table with his stuffed Spiderman backpack. Half the dishes from breakfast were scattered, as everyone had eaten and was now rushing around to get ready, everyone except Trevor, who was calm and appeared ready to go. It was always a transition, the first day back to school, from the lazy days of summer.

"Yes, Dad, all done." He always sounded so happy.

"Show me what you packed, bud." Brad rested his hand on Trevor's shoulder, and his son smiled that easy smile of his as he lifted out his lunch kit then gestured with the flat of his hand to the supplies he'd stuffed inside the backpack: folders, paper, and an orange pencil case. "What about your lunch? You made it yourself today. Show me what you did."

It took Trevor a minute, and then Emily rushed into the kitchen. "Trevor, come on, we have to go. Let me see what you packed." She reached for his lunch kit just as Trevor was about to unzip it.

"Em, I got it, honey. Go get the girls ready."

She gave him one of her harried looks as she ran around, trying to get everything done and everyone organized. As if right on schedule, frown lines appeared between her eyebrows.

"Aren't you the one who keeps telling me we have to let Trevor do it for himself or he'll never learn?" Brad said.

She rolled her eyes and sighed. "How about I trade with you? You deal with the girls, I'll take Trevor."

Trevor unzipped his lunch kit. "See here?" Again he gestured with the flat of his hand, looking up at Brad. His eyes had a sparkle of love that was so genuine. Emily went to reach in and lift out the two lunch containers and a Ziploc bag of broccoli.

"Em, let him do it," Brad said. "Besides, I'm taking the easy one today. You deal with the girls."

"Mom, I can't get the brush out of my hair," Becky cried as she raced into the kitchen, half dressed in a red skirt and pajama top, her long hair tangled in a round hair brush.

"What did you do?" Emily cried out as she touched the brush and tried pulling the knotted hair that was wrapped around the bristles.

"There's tuna, carrots, broccoli, an apple …" Trevor started just as Katy raced into the kitchen in her too-tight skinny jeans and a black and red floral shirt.

"Mom, my shoes! I can't find the new ones you bought. Someone took them!"

Emily looked as if she was going to lose it as she pointed to the back door. "Go and look in the shopping bag that's still sitting exactly where you left it four days ago. I told you I'm not your maid—"

Brad put his fingers in his mouth and gave a loud, sharp whistle. Everyone stopped. Even Trevor looked up at his dad, still holding the container with a rice wrap stuffed with tuna salad. "Katy, you're responsible for your own clothes and shoes," Brad said. "Your mom already made your lunch. Get moving. Becky, what did you do to your hair?"

"I wanted it all curled in ringlets for school, so I used Katy's gel in my hair and was blow drying it."

"You used my gel?" Katy yelled as she dragged a shopping bag from the back door, but she took one look at Brad's face and sighed. Maybe she knew she was skating on thin ice. Brad wasn't a pushover, and he certainly wasn't a mom. The kids thought they could vent and Emily would always be there to take it. "Okay, I'm going," Katy said.

"You've got less than five minutes, and then you go as you are," Brad called out after her. He set his hand on Trevor's shoulder. "Good job, Trevor. Pack it all back up, but you forgot an icepack for the sandwich. Where do you find those?"

Trevor smiled brightly as he looked up at his dad. "In the freezer?" he said, a twinkle in his eyes. Brad swore, at times, that Trevor was making fun of him.

"Yeah, go get it," he replied, shaking his head. He watched as Emily tried to untangle Becky's hair as the little girl screeched, "Mom, that hurts!"

"Can you get it out, or do you have to cut it?" Brad asked.

"I don't want my hair cut!" Becky was almost in tears.

"No, I won't cut it. I almost have it." She pulled the last piece out, but Becky's hair was a mess. "Go upstairs—we need to rinse this gel out. Of all the times to do this, Becky, when we're late to get out the door?"

Brad's calm and organized wife was quickly losing it. She sighed as she took Becky by the arm and hurried her upstairs, and Brad took in Trevor standing beside the table, happy.

Trevor gestured again to his lunch kit when Brad glanced his way. "There's the icepack. Can I zip it, Dad?"

Brad rustled his son's dark hair, which was brushed back on one side and forward on the other. He was neat and tidy in blue jeans and a green and blue striped shirt. "Well, at least you're ready for school. Pack it up, and let's go fix your hair. Remember to brush it back on both sides. Let's go try it again."

"Okay, Dad," Trevor said, and Brad followed his son—

the easy one, who grabbed hold of a routine and followed it without fail and without arguing. But everything he did had to be taught, and some days were easier than others. There were some days when Brad wondered whether he'd ever get it.

Chapter 3

Brad was waiting for Emily on the front steps when she parked his pickup. It was his brand new truck, a Dodge Ram with all the bells and whistles, and it had taken her some time to get used to driving it. Now that she had, she never wanted to drive the average, boring minivan everyone seemed to drive ever again. Brad complained endlessly about banging his knees when getting into the truck because she'd forget to move the seat back to accommodate his long legs each and every time.

As she walked around the front of the truck, he raised an eyebrow. He was leaning against the white pillar of the porch, holding a mug of coffee, wearing a red T-shirt, his faded blue jeans, and his cowboy boots, the ones he wore every day. He was the best-looking man Emily had ever seen.

"You're never going to drive that thing I bought you, are you?" Brad said, gesturing to the gray minivan, still shiny and new. She didn't think it had moved in a month.

She took a look at it before glancing back over to the

shiny black truck and shaking her head. "No. I like the truck better."

He had the most amazing smile. It started in his eyes and reached out to her, and it still had the ability to curl her toes. She started up the steps, and he opened his arms to her. This was her spot, beside him, and he didn't have to say a word as she slid right into his arms and snuggled against him. Breathing in his scent, male and earthy, always settled her when she was feeling lost and out of sorts—like today. She ran her hands around his waist, feeling the tightness of the muscles on his back, and she leaned in against the hard pillow of his chest. His arm was so steady and strong around her, and she listened as he took a swallow of coffee.

"So the kids are at school. All disasters have been averted, and there's peace and quiet now in your domain. So what do you think you're going to do with all your free time, Mrs. Friessen?"

She loved the way he teased, but he didn't have a clue what it took to run this house or raise his kids. Free time— was he kidding? "Trevor's birthday is coming up. He'll be the big thirteen. Any ideas on what we should do?"

"I can't believe how big he's getting," he replied, and she looked up at him. For a minute, there had been a shadow in his voice, but then it was gone, as if he needed to hide it from her. She wondered for a moment whether he was thinking of Trevor's mother, the woman who'd abandoned him, the woman who'd tried to destroy what Emily and Brad had. She wanted to kick herself every time thoughts of Crystal slipped into her mind. Brad's ex-wife was a darkness in the light and the only person who could threaten her happiness.

"He's looking more and more like you every day," she said. "He has your nose, your jaw, and the way he's filling out, he's already taller than me." But he had his mother's eyes, and his lips, the way he tightened them when he was angry, was all Crystal. She couldn't say that to Brad, though she knew he could see it too. "He's trying to sound like you. His voice is changing, and it's so cute when he uses that deep voice and tries to talk just like you. He looks up to you so much, Brad."

She could see the pride in his smile as he replied, "How about a party for him? We'll invite the family. Mom and Dad would love to come, and I spoke with Neil this morning when you took the kids to school."

She pulled away, wondering why he appeared bothered. "And what?" She nudged him with her arm around his waist.

He squinted as if the sun was shining in his eyes as he stared out to the yard, then shook his head. "Don't know what's going on with him."

Emily tapped her fingers on Brad's chest. "Can you share a little bit more? How's Candy—and Cat, the little girl they adopted, is she done with her surgeries? Come on, fill me in."

Brad actually squeezed her closer. "They have a baby. He called to tell me."

This time, she pulled away and took a step back. "Wow, I didn't expect that. After everything they went through with that surrogate, it just about ended their marriage. Tell me more. A baby? Wow."

"Yeah, wow is right. It's a boy, and he's three months old now."

The way Brad said it, she knew there was way more, and something about it was bothering him. "They just adopted him, or is it … ?" She didn't finish. Brad was shaking his head, clearly irritated with his brother.

"He's had the baby three months and is just telling me

now. Apparently Mom and Dad just found out, too. And, yes, Neil and Candy are still in Arizona with no plans to go back to Cancun."

Okay, that was odd. Wanting a baby so desperately had nearly torn Neil and Candy apart, and Neil had struggled like no man she'd ever seen when he realized Candy couldn't have children. She had wondered whether they'd make it or if he'd walk away. Some men just couldn't live with not having a child of their own, and she believed Neil was one of them. "Didn't you just talk to your brother last month?"

"Yes, and he didn't say one word about the baby. He sounded distracted, a little standoffish, but he said he had a lot on his mind with his resort. Things weren't going well. I thought he'd just overextended himself, and I offered to step in, but he said he'd be okay. I don't know what's going on with him."

"Maybe I should give Candy a call," Emily said. She was about to go, but Brad held tight.

"Maybe you shouldn't. If there's something going on … well, I know my brother. There's definitely something, and he doesn't need you and me sticking our noses in and stirring things up. Besides, I kind of went ahead and asked them to come out for Trevor's birthday. I'll feel him out then, sit down with him."

"You already invited people to a party we didn't even plan or decide on until a few moments ago?"

"They're not people, Emily. They're family." He said it a little sharply.

"What if I'd said no to the party?"

He raised his eyebrows. "Seriously, Em? You're the one always pushing for the family, for get-togethers, going outside of our comfort zone, and—what was your quote? —'thinking outside the box' for Trevor. Besides, when have you ever put up a wall in my family? I just figured a party would be great. Trevor can practice all he's learned, and you know how well he does around my family. You weren't considering saying no, were you?"

It irritated her, at times, how well he understood her—which was silly, because having a man like him was all she'd ever dreamed of. "No, but you phoned your brother and went ahead and invited him." She said it about the same time she felt all the wind go out of her accusation. "He called you, didn't he?"

"Yeah."

Of course, and it had probably just come up. She rested her head against him again. "Well, it'll be nice to see the baby and Cat and Candy again. They are coming, right?" She tilted her head up.

He smiled again. "Yeah."

He dumped out the rest of his coffee and ran his hand over her bottom, squeezing. She loved when he did that. "What do you say I finally take you upstairs for that good morning?" he asked.

She must have appeared shocked, as he mocked her by widening his eyes and mouth. He leaned in with a wicked smile and kissed her, jamming his hands in her hair, holding her as if he had every right to take her whenever and wherever he wanted. She loved the taste of him and how he knew just how to touch her, what to do to her, to have her screaming his name. She heard something shatter, but she barely registered the noise as he lifted her. She wrapped her legs around his waist, her arms linked around his neck, her breasts pressed against him. She wanted to tear his shirt off and feel him skin to skin, and she felt naughty and free. She couldn't believe what they were about to do in the middle of the day.

She giggled as he pulled open the door, holding her to

him and lifting his head just enough that she could see the fire and heat in his eyes, as if she was the only one who could stoke this passion in him. She could feel all his hardness and knew how much he wanted her as he pressed into her.

"So, no kids home … we can have animal sex. Maybe this is good," she said without thinking. He grinned again—wickedly. She kissed him deeper this time, tasting him. "And how long until your brother comes?"

He moved his lips down her neck, kissing and biting and then running his tongue over the tender skin. She was about to rip off her sweater and her T-shirt before he could take another step. "A couple days," he replied.

That stomped out the fire Brad had stoked in her. She thought of the mess in the spare room, where she had started cleaning out their junk last week. There was a mountain of work to get this house organized and rooms made up for his family. She swatted his shoulder and pushed away until he set her down.

"Two days, are you kidding me?" she said. "I can't have the house ready and make plans for Trevor's party that quickly. Why so soon? Trevor's birthday isn't for a week."

He actually went to reach for her again, but she swatted his hand away.

"Are you planning on helping me clean up?" she said, though it was a stupid question. Even if he did offer, he was the last person she wanted helping her organize. That was when they argued—*Which could be fun,* she thought, *especially the making-up part*—because his idea of cleaning and tidying was shoving everything into a closet and shutting the door. As he always said, "It's out of the way." No, hell no! She wanted to get rid of what they didn't need and find a better place for everything they were keeping.

"What's wrong with the place? It's neat and tidy." He gestured around the entryway.

"There's no place for your brother and Candy to sleep. They have a baby now, so you have to set up the crib again, which I'm pretty sure is still in pieces out in the barn from when you took it apart. Let's see … Cat can bunk in with Becky, because she has her daybed with a trundle underneath, but where will everyone else go? You're also planning on inviting your mom and dad. Need I say more?"

There was a knock at the back door. Then it opened, and there were heavy footsteps on the wood floor. "Hey, boss, we ran out of the de-wormer for the cows, and it looks like the extra bottle in the tack room was an empty someone shoved back in the box!" their foreman called out as he walked across the floor, his boots scraping the hardwood. Cliff poked his head through the archway into the living room. "Do you want me to run into town to get more, or do you want to do it?"

Brad actually reached into Emily's pocket and took his truck keys. "No, I'll go."

"Right-o," Cliff said before heading back out the door, slamming it behind him.

Brad looked miserable for a moment, sliding his hand under her chin and holding her face still. "Tonight, you're going to make this up to me, my cold morning and this lost opportunity, so don't you dare overdo it today." Then he kissed her again, hard and possessively, sliding his tongue into her mouth, tasting her, before pulling away, leaving her breathless and shaky. Brad held up his keys. "And I'm taking my truck," he stated before starting out the front door.

She watched him walk away, her husband in his faded Levi's … with the most amazing ass she'd ever seen. She leaned against the wall as the truck engine started, already planning and putting together lists and errands, trying to figure out what she needed to do first.

Chapter 4

"Jed, I'm sorry. Let Diana know we wish her well," Brad said before hanging up the phone.

Emily took in his expression as she stirred the chili simmering on the burner. "They can't come?" she said.

Brad shook his head. "Diana's come down with a cold—Danny and Christopher, too. It's gone through the house. Jed said he'd bring them for a visit as soon as they're better, but he isn't holding out much hope for the party on Friday."

She could see the disappointment on his face. He was bothered that his whole family couldn't be here, and she couldn't help but feel bad. She'd been feeling overwhelmed completely, what with organizing the house, cleaning out the extra bedrooms upstairs, and trying to figure out where everyone would sleep. (At this point, with Diana and Jed not coming, Rodney and Becky would be left in Katy's room, taking her queen bed, and Neil and Candy would be in the spare room with the double, where Brad had already set up the crib. The three girls, Becky, Katy, and Cat, would sleep in little Becky's room, and Trevor would get to keep his.) She actually let out a big sigh.

"I can see you're relieved," he said, coming up behind her and rubbing her back and her shoulders. Even through his touch, she sensed his disappointment.

"I'm not relieved. I'm bothered that I'm worrying about where to put everyone, and I know this is so important to you. I'm sorry. You know I love your family." She sighed again as she tried to let go of all her worried energy. "You know it'll be good for Trevor to have them here, too." She tapped the wooden spoon on the edge of the pot and set it down on the stove, then leaned against Brad and slid her arms around his waist, letting him hug her. He rested his chin on top of her head. She loved it when he held her like this.

"Dinner ready?" Katy rushed in, Becky chattering nonstop behind her.

Outside, a car door slammed shut.

Brad pulled away, and Emily frowned as she heard voices. "You expecting someone?" he asked.

The girls raced ahead out the door, chattering away. Emily knew before she and Brad reached the screen door that Neil and Candy were here, as she could hear everyone's excitement at the reunion. Brad pushed open the screen door, still holding her hand, and she followed him out.

Neil and Candy stood beside a midsize black car with Arizona plates. The back door was open, and the girls were hugging Neil and then leaning into the backseat to, she presumed, look at the baby.

"I thought Neil was coming tomorrow?" she said to Brad, but he was shaking his head. He, too, wore an odd expression.

"That's what he told me," he said quietly. He squeezed their linked fingers, and she touched his arm and followed him as he called out across the yard, "We weren't expecting you until tomorrow!" He started down the steps, his hand sliding from Emily's as he hugged his brother, patting his back.

"Neil loaded us up in the car after he talked to you, Brad," Candy said. "We didn't know how far we'd get, driving with the baby." She was standing by the open back door, a huge smile on her face. She looked different, wearing blue jeans and a pale knit shirt, her long dark hair tied back in a ponytail. She was lovely, with her complexion and brown eyes. She appeared so relaxed, and there was something else different, too—something Emily had never seen in her before.

"So you made good time," Emily said as she stepped toward Neil and hugged him. His hug was unusually tight, and it lingered. When she pulled away, she realized Brad had been right: Neil wasn't himself. But then, they had a new baby, as well as a little girl who'd needed to receive cochlear implants, and they had moved all the way to Arizona. They seemed to be in flux. Maybe that was what she was picking up on. "The baby was good at traveling?" she asked.

Neil glanced at Candy, who was calm and confident. She squeezed in between the girls and lifted out a baby from the backseat. She wore the brightest smile as she gazed down at him, kicking and reaching for her finger as he let out a sweet baby giggle.

"Oh, let me see him!" Emily said. "What's his name?" She took in the baby, who was dressed in a light blue sleeper, a striped green and white blanket wrapped around him. He had dark hair and a round face, with tiny lips, pale skin, and light brown eyes.

"This is Michael," Candy said as Neil started around the other side of the vehicle and opened the back door. Emily could hear him talking to Cat as he lifted her out. They had adopted the little dark-haired girl from a Mexican orphanage. She wrapped her arms around Neil's neck and appeared sleepy, just staring at everyone. The girls were chattering a mile a minute to Neil, and Cat rested her head against his shoulder. Her short hair didn't quite touch her shoulders, and it was sticking up here and there, a little messy, probably from the long car ride. Neil kissed her forehead, and she gripped his blue sweater with her tiny fist. Any fool could see the love he had for her. There was so much going on among Neil, Candy, and their new family that Emily was stuck trying to sort it out in her mind. The fact that he wasn't reaching for the baby—more intent on holding a little girl Emily knew he hadn't originally wanted—made her take a closer look at him.

"How's she doing after the surgery?" Brad asked. He put his hands on Katy and Becky's shoulders and snuggled them to each side of him.

"She's doing good, had a follow-up last week. Everything looks good, no infection, and the implant's working. She's working with a speech and language therapist," Neil replied, rubbing her back.

This was a side of her brother-in-law that Emily hadn't expected to see. If she'd ever had any doubt about his feelings for the little girl, she didn't anymore.

"She doesn't have her cochlear implant attached right now," Neil explained. He signed something to her, and she lifted her head, rubbed her eyes, and signed something back. He kissed her on the forehead again. "She doesn't want it back on right now. She said it's itchy."

"Brad, the chili!" Emily suddenly cried, realizing the

burner was still on. She hoped there would be enough for dinner. Maybe she'd throw another salad together, and there were buns in the freezer, too. Her mind was racing.

"We didn't call to let you know we were coming this early, so I hope we haven't messed up your dinner plans," Candy said.

Brad was shaking his head. "Candy, there's one thing about my wife that's an absolute given: She always makes sure there's more than enough to go around and then some. She'll never admit this, but I figured it out a long time ago. She does it just in case someone shows up. We're always packing the fridge with leftovers. Katy, run in and turn the burner off for your mom," he said, patting Katy's shoulder.

Even though Katy was from Emily's first marriage, Brad was her father. She'd called him Dad ever since they were married. It was just a given. He loved her and scolded her and reprimanded her. He was the first real father figure she'd had.

"Okay" was all she said before racing into the house, the screen door slapping closed behind her.

"Come on, Becky. You can help carry something in." Brad popped the trunk, grabbed a suitcase, and started for the house. "Dinner's probably ready, so I hope you're hungry!"

Whatever Neil said to Brad, Emily couldn't make it out. They were laughing, following Becky to the house. Trevor had appeared in the doorway. She could see him through the screen door. Brad said something to him, and he said "Okay" in a strong voice. Neil teased him about something, and he laughed.

"Your dad tell you to help carry stuff in?" Emily said as he approached her.

"Yes, he did, Mom," Trevor said, walking with confidence in each step. He stopped at the trunk, looking in, before lifting out one small bag and starting back to the house.

"Hey, wait a second! You have two arms." She jutted her chin toward the trunk when he made a face. "Grab a second bag and carry it."

"Okay," he said with a heavy sigh, as if it was such an effort, before grabbing a plastic shopping bag.

Emily was still holding the baby, and Candy was reaching into the car and lifting out a diaper bag.

"He's probably wet. I should change him," she explained, lingering for a minute beside Emily with an odd expression on her face. She glanced to the door Trevor had gone through.

"So, how are you two?" Emily asked.

Candy smiled, looking at her with such happiness. Then she sighed. "We're good, actually," she said. Maybe she didn't think Emily believed her, as she widened her eyes with an intense expression Emily had never seen before. She reached for her baby and took him from Emily comfortably, beaming down at him as he cooed up at her. "We're in a place now that I didn't expect. I have my husband back. I don't even know how to explain how close we are. I never thought it could be possible. He loves Cat so much—and me, I know without a doubt what I mean to him. Being in Arizona, just us, it feels as if he's keeping everything and everyone away from us, from our family, to protect us. I love it. It's just …"

She bit her lower lip, glancing from the door to Emily. "After everything we went through because Neil wanted a baby, with that surrogate..." She shut her light brown eyes as if trying to rid herself of a bad memory. When she opened them, they were filled with a new lightness. Emily liked this new version of Candy, but sadness still lingered in her expression. "I expected Neil to be all over this baby," she said.

"And he's not?" Emily, too, glanced toward the door. She could see Brad and Neil talking there, about to come out and finish unloading the car.

Candy shook her head. "No, he's more focused on Cat: holding her, reading to her…doing whatever he can for her. He leaves the baby to me. Maybe it's because it's not his." She shook her head, and Emily could see her confusion. "I don't know, I'm just guessing. I've asked him if everything's all right, and he says everything's fine— perfect, even. Maybe I'm making too much out of it, because we've never been closer. He's so …" She actually blushed. Emily glanced to the door again.

"Really?" she asked. She didn't need Candy to fill in the blanks to know how possessive Neil was … and to know what she meant by "closer." If Neil was anything like Brad, he had Candy flat on her back, with him buried inside her, at every opportunity.

"He's always touching me. Every time I look, he's watching me from across the room, and at night … I never expected it to be this good between us. I've never in my life felt so connected to someone, to Neil. I feel as if he's a part of me. If I had any doubts about how much he loves me, I don't now."

"Candy?" Neil called out as he started down the steps. "I'll grab the rest of the bags. Go inside with Emily. Brad's just putting dinner on the table." Neil reached for her and put both hands on her cheeks, leaning in to kiss her. The baby fussed between them, and he only glanced down before looking at his wife again. Emily could see what

Candy meant about Neil loving her—anyone around them would wonder whether they were newlyweds—but she could also see that Neil seemed to show no interest in the baby at all. Candy had seen that, too, but as she tucked the blanket around Michael and whispered something to him lovingly, she appeared not to give it a second thought.

Chapter 5

"Are they getting settled?" Emily asked as she flicked her gaze over to Brad, who was wiping down the kitchen table. Katy was rinsing the dishes, and Trevor was loading the dishwasher. Cat and Becky were upstairs with Neil.

"Candy is just getting the baby settled, and Neil said he's going to throw both girls in the bath together."

"Trevor, don't put Mom's pot in like that or the dishwasher won't work," Katy started.

"But it's fine. It's in." He gestured to the large pot stacked on top of the plates.

"Take it out, please," Emily said. "Katy, you know better. That needs to be washed by hand. Don't leave it in the pile for Trevor."

Brad watched Katy with Trevor. She was so good with him and so close in age, too. Like all of them, she knew how to talk to Trevor, but she also pushed his buttons at times.

"Mom, what's next?" Trevor asked as Katy lifted out the pot and started filling the sink, sulking.

"You and Katy finish loading the dishwasher, start it, and then wipe the counters down. Make sure all the food is in the fridge. Wash everything else by hand—all the pots, too, Katy. I'm not kidding, you two. Trevor, you dry and make sure everything's put away in the fridge, covered. Don't stack the heavy things on top of the light things or they'll tip over."

Emily actually had to take a breath. Trevor was holding a dish towel, not paying her any mind, but he said, "Okay, Mom, stop worrying."

Brad wondered at what point in her mini-tirade his son had tuned her out. "Yeah, Mom, stop worrying," he murmured, taking her hand. "Come on, let the kids finish."

She hesitated for a minute. He could see the wheels turning in her mind as if she needed to find a reason to stay and supervise. Then she sighed and dropped the sponge on the table. "You're right. I just …"

He didn't let her finish as he tugged her hand, pulling her from the kitchen. "I know you want to stay and supervise, but you need to let them finish without standing over them," Brad said as he dragged her out onto the front porch and settled on the cushioned deck chair, pulling Emily onto his lap.

"You weren't the one who had to clean up the fridge after they put dinner away last night. They stuck the soup pot on top of two tiny plastic containers, and it dumped over everything. It took me an hour last night to empty the fridge and clean it out."

Brad pulled her in closer until he felt her relax against him. "If they make a mess, you make them clean it up. You're not their maid. Aren't you the one who's always telling me to stop making things easier and doing everything for Trevor? It applies to the girls, too, Emily. Those two are starting to run circles around you."

He could feel her tense before she swatted at his shoulder. "Yes, I did, but it's easier said than done. I sometimes find it easier to just do it myself, especially with the girls."

"Isn't that exactly what Trevor's consultant told us not to do? Really, those two girls should be doing a lot more than they are."

She was perched on his leg in her low-rise blue jeans and a green shirt that was buttoned up high enough to give him only a glimpse of her cleavage, enough to tease him, hinting at what he had to look forward to when they went to bed. "Yes, she did. Point taken, Brad. He's doing so well. I just want him to keep doing well, and with the girls … I know you're right," she said, twirling her wedding band around her finger.

"He is doing well," Brad said. "God, every day, Em, I see the difference in him. He makes his bed, puts his clothes in the laundry, gets dressed himself, packs his lunch, brushes his teeth, cleans up. He's better than the girls."

"I know he is." She slid her arm around his neck and rested her head on his shoulder. "He's so amazing. I mean, look how far he's come. We're so lucky. He has no bad behavior, and he's so happy, quickly grasping what he's learning. I realized that the other day, when I showed him how to do laundry, I forgot to show him how to separate darks and lights. He put it all in together, and that was my fault, but once I went through it with him again and showed him, I couldn't believe how quickly he got it. He's asking to do laundry all the time now. He even started making Katy's bed for her. Becky's, too. I'm going to have to talk to the girls, as they're letting him. With the girls, it feels as if I have to crack the whip to get them to follow through."

Brad snorted. "Yeah, and that's got to stop. We'll sit down with them, and I'll lay down the law with those two."

She started to sit up again. "Really, Brad, the law?"

"It's time, Em. Seriously, I'm not having the kids running you ragged anymore. They need more responsibility. You spoil the girls, and we also need to talk about busing, Em. Trevor's ready to get on now, and Katy will be there this year for middle school. Becky's fine to ride the bus, too."

"I know. Just give me a week to get used to the idea so I can talk to the bus driver first about Trevor."

He knew she was worried, and he couldn't rush her, not with something like this, but at least now she could get used to the idea. He held her and sat in a comfortable silence, listening to the sounds in the house. "Did you notice anything off about my brother?" Brad said. He wondered whether Emily had picked up on Neil's indifference toward the baby. It wasn't that it was a huge deal, as Candy had surprised the hell out of him with how comfortable she was with Michael, feeding him and holding him. She even seemed less nervous with Trevor, Katy, and Becky. The last time she had been there was for her and Neil's wedding, and she'd been terrified around the kids. She was relaxed now, or so it seemed, but Neil seemed the polar opposite. Brad wondered what was really going on there.

"Yes, I noticed, but I didn't want to say anything to you. It almost seems as if he doesn't want the baby, but I don't understand how that can be. I mean, have you seen him with Candy, the love that's there? I'm glad they've worked things out, as they seem closer than I've ever seen them, but I think you should talk to Neil. Something's wrong," Emily said in a low voice.

"And how do you know that?" Brad asked, though they

were clearly thinking the same thing.

"Call it women's intuition, but something's going on with Neil. He and Candy have had a hard road, with painful moments most couples wouldn't have gotten past. Their relationship has been far from easy."

There was giggling and footsteps, then Neil's laughter. He pushed open the screen door. Becky was giggling, bathed and dressed in her flower nightgown, and Neil was carrying Cat, who was in teddy bear pajamas, a big grin on her face.

"I'm putting these two troublemakers to bed," Neil said. Cat had her cochlear implant fastened behind her ear, and she giggled at the odd sound of his voice. "I'm going to read them a couple stories. Is Katy bunking in with them tonight?"

"Thursday we'll move her out of her room and set up an air mattress on the floor. Mom and Dad are flying in Thursday morning," Brad said.

Neil's expression darkened at the mention of his parents. All the teasing and lightness that had been in his expression a moment ago was gone. "Okay, I've got two, maybe three books to read to these two monkeys, and then I'm putting them to bed." The girls giggled again, and Neil started back into the house.

"Neil, does Candy need anything upstairs for the baby?" Emily asked, leaning her head back on Brad's shoulder.

He didn't even look at them. "I'll check on Candy to see if she needs anything, but the baby's fine."

As he left, Emily gave Brad a look. "You need to have a talk with your brother."

"Tomorrow" was all he said, hoping that after a good night's sleep, Neil would be back to his old self.

Chapter 6

"Neil, do you think you could take the baby? I need a shower," Candy said as she walked into the kitchen the next morning in a light pink robe. Her hair was tangled, and she looked tired. The kids were at the table, shoveling cereal into their mouths, and Brad was filling a go-mug with coffee.

Emily took in Neil, standing behind Cat at the table with his damp hair, dark jeans, and a dark green knit shirt. He was unshaven, with maybe two or three days' growth, which was unlike him. He was the only one of the brothers to never have that shaggy look going on, even though it was damn attractive. He set a glass of juice in front of Cat and then rubbed her dark hair. She smiled up at him, her papa, as he walked over to the counter and put down his mug. Emily didn't miss the slight hesitation when he glanced over to Candy. She wouldn't have noticed if she hadn't been watching so closely, but she was beginning to see things about him, his tension. He was holding something back every time he was around the baby.

"Candy, the baby had you up a lot last night," Emily

remarked as she dumped oats into a pot of water on the stove.

"I'm so sorry if he woke you up! I brought him downstairs and rocked him so he wouldn't disturb anyone, but I think with all the traveling, he wasn't too interested in sleeping last night," Candy replied. Her voice was tired and scratchy.

Neil didn't say a word at first, taking the baby from her in one arm and sliding his other around her shoulders. "Go get in the shower, and then why don't you go back to bed and get some sleep?" He leaned in and kissed her, and Emily noticed he didn't give Michael a second look. The baby started to fuss, picking up on Neil's indifference.

Brad must have noticed, too, as he set his coffee mug down and went over to his brother. "Come here, Michael. Let me have a look at you." He actually scooped the baby from Neil, who steered Candy out of the kitchen and up the stairs. Brad gave Emily a sharp glance. She was about to say something when Neil hurried back into the kitchen. Michael was starting to fuss again, his tiny fists waving in the air, but Neil didn't even glance his way as he walked past his brother, going for his coffee instead.

Emily stared at Brad. He was looking at the baby and patting his bottom as he glanced over at her again. She knew he'd seen it, too.

"Hey, Neil, why don't you give me a hand this morning with the cattle?" Brad said. He smacked his brother on the shoulder, and Neil shrugged.

"Sure."

Sure? She was trying to get her head around Neil's response. It was so … off. Brad, as he walked straight toward her, had a look in his eyes that told her he was taking his brother out to have that much-needed talk with him now.

"Em, take the baby," Brad said quietly, sliding Michael into her arms. He was such a good baby, but he was a little fussy this morning, and she still had to make breakfast and get the kids ready for school. Maybe her expression showed what she was thinking, as Brad leaned in and kissed her. "Trevor, come stir this on the stove for your mom," he said, as if that was going to help.

"Okay, Dad." Trevor slid back his chair and wiped his face with his shirt sleeve, walking over to the stove and taking the wooden spoon from Emily. He put it in the pot as the oats bubbled.

"That's it—in a circle. Hold the pot handle with your other hand," Emily said absently, listening to Brad and Neil's footsteps as they started out the door. "After breakfast, you need to change your shirt."

"Okay, Mom," Trevor said as he kept stirring.

NEIL CUT the twine on a bale of hay and tossed it into the wooden feeder for the cows. Brad leaned against the fence rail, watching as the cows moved in to grab a mouthful of hay from between the slats.

Neil's feet squished in the mud. He'd changed into a pair of Brad's gumboots in the barn while helping him load up the gator with the bales of hay. Brad just watched as his brother ran his fingers through hair that was a little on the long side for Neil. He was wearing an average black all-weather coat, which was also unlike him. Brad had expected Neil to arrive in his usual leather, high end and expensive.

"So what's going on?" Brad finally asked, watching his brother's expression. It was closely guarded, and his eyes didn't meet Brad's.

Neil shrugged. "Nothing's going on. Why would you ask?" he said in a tone that was supposed to sound light but instead came out as forced.

"I'm your brother, Neil. I know you well enough to know something is going on. Something or someone is messing with you or has messed with you. Which is it?"

Neil stopped at the rail and leaned on it, looking away from Brad as if lost in thought. He said nothing.

"Candy looks good," Brad said. "She seems happy." He could see that just the mention of Candy brought a smile to his brother's face. When Neil looked his way again, there was something in his expression that told Brad his brother would walk through fire for Candy. But there was something else, too, and he couldn't put his finger on it.

"She's a great mother," Neil said. "I love her so much. I don't deserve her."

Well, that was definitely not what he'd been expecting. Neil was the most confident, arrogant, and shamelessly cocky one of all the Friessen boys. He was also known for being direct, and avoiding eye contact was something he'd never done. This visit, avoiding and hiding were things Neil had done with him repeatedly.

Neil cleared his throat as he moved over beside Brad at the rail. "I'm thinking of moving us up this way, buying a place close to you. Do you think Dad would buy me out?"

For a minute, all Brad could do was blink. "You're moving up here now? Why wouldn't you just *ask* Dad to buy you out? You two are close … or did something happen?" he asked. Neil started to move as if he was going to walk away, so Brad reached out and grabbed his shoulder. "Hey, what the hell, Neil? Look, this is me. Whatever it is, you know you can tell me. I'm not a fool. I can see something's going on, and whatever it is has got you twisted up inside."

For a moment, Neil's face was so grief stricken and desolate that Brad was flooded with worry. Neil shut his eyes and fisted his hands. When he opened them back up, they shook as he jammed his fingers through his hair and pulled, as if that was the only way he could get the words out.

"Are you in trouble?" Brad said. "Did you kill someone? What the hell, Neil?" He was almost growling. He'd never seen his brother like this, and for a minute he suspected that his brilliant, self-made brother, who was the problem solver in the family, had gotten himself into the kind of trouble he wouldn't be able to find his way out of.

"I did something, and if Candy ever finds out, I don't think she'll forgive me," Neil said. "I can't lose her."

"Whatever you did, it can't be that bad, Neil," Brad began. He reached for his brother's shoulder and squeezed, but Neil let out a harsh grunt. He was doing everything he could to hold it together.

"Oh, it's worse," he said. "You know when you lie, and instead of coming clean, you just keep digging a hole? Pretty soon it's so big and dark that it's a grave you can't get out of. I lied about the baby." Neil looked directly at Brad, and his brown eyes, usually filled with light, were dull and sad. "The baby's mine."

Chapter 7

He wasn't sure he'd heard his brother correctly. Neil was looking out to the field as if he wished he were anywhere but standing beside Brad.

"The baby is yours," Brad said quietly. He was holding himself still, his arms across his chest, his mind working. How was this possible? Then he remembered the surrogate … or was there someone else?

Neil didn't say anything. When he looked at Brad, he was unrecognizable.

"How is this baby yours? You had a surrogate—or did you cheat?" Even saying it left a bitter taste in his mouth. The Friessens weren't cheaters. They were about family, they loved their wives, and Brad wouldn't hesitate to knock his brother around if he learned he'd messed with another woman.

"I would never cheat," Neil snapped. "I may have done a lot of things, Brad, and I may be a miserable excuse for a husband, but that's a line I would never cross. Candy's my wife, and I love her. I made a vow to her, a promise. The baby is from Maria, the surrogate. I lied, okay?" he shouted, his arms out wide as if he was telling the world.

Brad just stared at his brother. "You said she lost the baby. You told your wife that," he said. Then he realized Neil had never come out and told him that, not exactly. He'd never even said much about the surrogate at all. "What gives, Neil? This isn't you. You had tunnel vision with having a baby, we all saw it, and we worried about what you were going to get yourself into. Why would you lie? Candy knew about the surrogate. We all did. I don't understand why you would do that!"

"Because I was so obsessed with having a baby that I didn't see what was happening right in front of me." Neil took a step and then faced Brad. "I moved her into the house, and Candy left."

Brad took a breath, about to say something, then stopped. "Maybe you should start at the beginning."

"You knew I had a surrogate."

"Yes, we did," Brad said, glancing toward the cows crowding the feeder.

"I was so fixated on having a baby, my baby, my blood, that I didn't see all the problems that came along with using a surrogate. Candy did. I didn't listen." He shook his head. "Maria and her mother … those two were quite a combination. Maria was nice, eager—too eager. Then she started spotting, and the doctor put her on bed rest. What I didn't tell Candy was that Maria's mother insisted I move her in with us. I had given them money to support themselves, but Maria's mother refused to look after her. She said she had to go with me, as it would be the only way to ensure that Maria stayed in bed. So I moved her in, and I didn't ask Candy. I just … I was angry with her because of all the time she spent at the orphanage." Neil sat on a stump and rested his elbows on his knees.

"With Cat—she spent all her time with Cat, and you were angry?" Brad said.

"Yeah."

"Because … come on, help me out here, Neil. I'm having a really hard time figuring this out."

"Because I wanted her at home, with me, excited about the baby, sharing it all with me—*me!*" he yelled again, now standing in the mud. "I know I'm a selfish bastard."

"You wanted to control her, tell her what to do, what to think. Is that what you're saying? Because it sure sounds like it to me."

Neil sneered in a way that wasn't flattering. "You think you're any different from me? I've seen you with Emily."

"Oh, you're so wrong," Brad snapped. "I know how strong willed I am, but so's my lovely wife. I protect her and my kids, if that comes across to you as controlling, then I feel sorry for you. My wife has me wrapped around her finger, and she knows I'll do anything for her and my kids. There's a difference between what you did and how I am with Emily—but you're right about one thing, Neil. That was damn selfish of you, shoving another woman in her face."

The fire that sparked in Neil's amber eyes was like nothing Brad had ever seen. For a minute, he thought his brother was going to lose it. Then Neil turned away, shaking his head.

"I know it was selfish. You think it makes me feel any better to have you tell me?"

"So why the secrecy, the story, the lies? Just come clean. Why not just follow through with the baby and be done with it?"

"Because I went too far. When she left, it was bad— really bad. I watched her pull away, and I was so angry and hurt. I truly believed that was it, that it was over. Nothing mattered at that moment. Then I got into it with Dad, and I had to hear from my own father that I'd fucked up by moving another woman into the house. Dad pointed out that Maria was in love with me and that Candy knew it. He told me to move her out, whatever it took, or I'd have to make a choice between my wife and the surrogate. Dad reminded me that one of the things he'd taught us was that a Friessen man lived and died by his word, and I'd made a promise to Candy when I married her."

Brad didn't know what to say. His dad had said nothing, but then, Rodney wasn't a man to talk about anyone's business.

"But when Jim came to the door …" Neil started. Maybe he realized, by the confused expression on his face, that Brad didn't have any idea who Jim was. "A pediatrician in Mexico who Candy met. He was in love with my wife. I opened the door, and he sucker punched me, knocked the wind out of me. I was ready to kill him, but that bastard yelled in my face that I didn't deserve her, saying how badly I'd hurt her by shoving Maria in her face. Candy believed I was replacing Maria with her. God, as if I could ever replace her! It was the wake-up call I needed, and it hurt to know she was confiding in another man. I couldn't let him have her, and I was driving her right toward him—all because of Maria.

"Then there was Cat. Do you have any idea how low a bastard I am? I'm absolutely ashamed of myself. I pray that little girl never finds out how much I hated her then, believing she was responsible for all my problems with Candy. She was a sweet, innocent little girl who couldn't hear and who no one gave a damn about until my wife found her rotting, tossed away in that orphanage." Neil was shaking his head again, his eyes glistening with tears.

Brad couldn't figure out what to say. Neil was hard-headed like all of them, but he'd always been the one with everything figured out: the most reasonable, the problem solver, the negotiator. None of this sounded like his brother.

"I went to Maria, who was lying in bed in the bedroom across from the one I shared with my wife, and it was then that I took a really hard look at what I'd done," Neil said. "Seeing the open door of her bedroom across the hall, Candy had it thrown in her face every time she came home. It was cruel, and I said to Maria that I was moving her out and hiring a nurse to be with her. I realized then that she held all the cards—always had. She said she was in love with me. She could give me the children my wife couldn't. Then she threatened to keep the baby, saying the laws in Mexico wouldn't honor a surrogacy contract. Smart woman, did her homework—or her mother did. All along, she'd been changing things. She didn't want the counseling ..." He stopped talking and shut his eyes again.

"I bought her a house, her and her mother. I moved her out, and there were tears and threats, then pleading. I left her and went after my wife, and I made arrangements for Cat, and I moved us to Arizona for her surgery. That was when you and Emily came to visit."

"I don't know what to say, Neil. Why didn't you tell me what was going on?"

"Because I tried to bury it! I cut all contact with Maria and focused on my wife, trying to rebuild our life together. During the surgeries for Cat, I fell in love with that precious little girl." There were tears in Neil's eyes, a passion Brad had never seen before. "I pushed all thoughts of the baby from my mind. It was easier to tell Candy that Maria had lost the baby. It just came out, because I couldn't stand to see the hurt in her eyes and know I was responsible for putting it there. I felt it was the only way to get my wife back, but I didn't think it through, because my lawyer called when Maria had the baby. She demanded to see me, and I said no."

"I don't understand, then, how you got Michael if she was using the baby to get to you."

"I paid her off, Brad. Five million dollars to sign away her rights and walk away. It was all I had left after building the resort. I gladly gave it to her to get her the hell out of my life," Neil said. "Don't look at me like that, Brad. You're no different from me."

"The hell I'm not."

Neil jabbed his finger toward him. "Really, brother dear? Exactly how much did you pay Trevor's birth mother to go away forever?"

Brad shoved Neil and even raised his fist before pulling it back and holding his hands out. "You asshole, what happened with Crystal wasn't the same thing at all." He started to walk away when Neil called out.

"You sure about that, Brad? From where I'm standing, you paid a woman to sign away her rights, the same as I did. The circumstances may have been different, but it was still to rectify a fucked-up mess you created."

Brad didn't turn around. At that moment, he was sure he would seriously hurt his brother if he didn't keep walking.

Chapter 8

When Brad came back inside with Neil for breakfast, he was a different man. His entire demeanor and expression was dark. Emily touched his arm and felt him instantly stiffen. When she tried to pull him aside, he was unusually brusque, and when he looked deeply at her, she could see anger simmering below the surface of his intense gaze. He was trying to sort something through in his mind. "Not now," he said, and she knew by how he stood there, watching her, that Brad was now in the loop with whatever was going on with Neil—and he wasn't about to share it with her.

"Enough!" he yelled at both Becky and Katy, who started nagging Emily when they couldn't find first their shoes and then their backpacks. He was short tempered, and it soon became clear that Dad wasn't about to be pushed around this morning. "Get yourselves organized, and stop bugging your mom," he said firmly. Emily didn't see this kind of take-no-shit attitude in Brad often, and neither did the kids, but they all knew Dad meant business.

They hustled and got themselves ready without another complaint.

Neil had taken Cat and the baby upstairs, and even then Brad just shook his head when Emily tried to ask him what was going on. Again he said, "Not now. We have Mom and Dad coming in late this afternoon and a party tomorrow." He brushed back his jacket, resting his hand on his hip. "Write down what you need me to pick up in town for the party." He actually tapped the counter with his finger.

"Brad, I want to know what's going on," she whispered, putting her hand on his arm, but he had a look about him that made her think he was ready to snap. She'd always been able to reason with him, but this Brad, this morning, wasn't even close to being reasonable.

He just held her gaze for a minute then shook his head. "Drop it, okay?" he said quite sharply. She couldn't remember him ever talking to her like that.

Maybe she flinched, because he let out a breath and brushed her cheek with the palm of his hand. His face was tight. "Don't, Em. There are some things … just don't." He couldn't even finish the sentence, but he leaned in and kissed her. It was nothing tender and passionate, but it was enough to let her know he loved her. When he pulled away, she knew that whatever Neil shared had to have been pretty bad to do this to her husband.

He tapped the counter again and took his truck keys from the hook. "You've got your minivan today." He held up his keys. "I'm taking the truck." Then he was gone.

"Ready to go, Mom?" Trevor was standing in the doorway, his coat on, his backpack ready, his hair combed neatly, and his shoes on the wrong feet.

She sighed, looking at Trevor, a boy she thought of as her own, who'd come so far but still had miles to go.

Brad took a moment to settle his thoughts as he leaned against his truck, taking in the blue sky and thick clouds beginning to roll in. He could see the approaching aircraft his mom and dad were flying in on, but instead of feeling the excitement of having most of his family together to celebrate Trevor's birthday, he was feeling an undercurrent of trouble brewing.

Brad didn't know what had been going through his brother's head, creating this volatile situation that could destroy everything he'd built. He wanted to shake him. He didn't know what to say to Neil, as he was still trying to understand what had driven him to create this lie about his son. He'd dug himself so deep into this hole, believing it was the only way to keep his wife—at least, Brad thought that was his motivation. The thing was that Neil hadn't even told Brad why he'd done it.

He was seeing his brother in a way he never had before, and it wasn't good. The last thing he wanted was for Neil to lose everything he'd fought for and built with Candy. They'd had such a hard road, coming together after every shitty curve ball that had been thrown at them. There was love there, but there was something about deceit and lies that could destroy everything. Brad knew this all too well, having once been married to a deceitful, dishonest woman: his first wife, Crystal, who'd given birth to Trevor and then abandoned him. He hated her still, and Brad couldn't stop himself from worrying that Neil was destroying everything good in his life, and Candy … well, she might never be able to forgive him if she found out. Worse, Brad found himself complicit in the lie just by knowing about it.

He could see his parents disembarking a small

commuter aircraft, and he hurried inside the small square building just as they followed another passenger through the glass doors.

"Hey, Mom, Dad, glad you could come." Brad hugged his mother and then reached for his dad's hand, pulling him into a hug and slapping his back. "Dad, you had a good flight?"

"Smooth. Had a bit of a panic transferring in Seattle, though. They couldn't find your mother's bag."

"They did, though," his mom said, appearing a little tired. She pulled her light brown jacket on and shivered. "Colder here."

"Fall weather, Mom, not as warm as Cancun. You're going a little soft," Brad teased. For the first time, he noticed the extra lines on his mother's face. They were both getting older, his mother seventy this year. In the few months since he'd last seen her, she seemed as if she'd aged, though his dad appeared the same.

"So is your brother here?" his father asked, and Brad almost asked which one. He caught himself, as he knew darn well it was Neil that Rodney was referring to.

He let out a sigh that seemed to translate to "I'm so done with all this crap" even to his own ears. "Neil and Candy are here with the new baby and Cat, if that's who you're referring to."

His mom and dad exchanged an odd expression. "Rodney, don't," his mom said, and of course Brad wondered what was going on now.

"Well, maybe we should clear the air before we go home," Brad said. "I don't want the kids picking up on whatever this tension is. This is about Trevor's birthday, and if you and Neil are going to start something, he'll notice."

Rodney gave Brad a hard look. "Look, I don't know how much you know——"

"Dad, I know way more than I want to," he interrupted. "Having said that, it's probably not even half the story. Right now, I want to go home and help my wife get ready for Trevor's party tomorrow."

Maybe his mom understood, because she reached out and patted his arm. "Help your dad with the bags," she said, then went out of the small airport and waited out front.

"What's going on with Mom? She looks tired, older," Brad said as he grabbed one of the luggage carts to start loading up their suitcases.

"This thing with Neil and Candy, it's taken its toll on your mom."

Brad just nodded and glanced out to where his mother stood waiting. "Look, I don't want to get into it with you, Dad, but Neil is a big boy, and he has to figure things out himself. How about we just have a good time for Trevor, and then you can take Neil aside and have at him?"

His dad put his hand on his shoulder and stopped him. "Hey, I'm not about to start anything. We're here to see our grandkids and to celebrate Trevor's birthday. I understand he's doing so much better. This is a celebration, right?"

"Right."

Brad loaded up the bags and tossed them in the back of his truck as his parents settled in the cab. He just couldn't shake the feeling that this weekend would be anything but the happy celebration they'd planned. And, boy, did he hope he was wrong.

$$\mathit{Chapter\ 9}$$

Emily came out of their bathroom just as Brad shut the door to their bedroom. He unbuttoned his brown shirt and pulled it free from the waistband of his jeans, and he still seemed distracted.

"The kids asleep?" she asked, feeling the silk camisole skim her thighs. It was the backless cream one—indecent, and it should have caught his full attention. She stepped closer, the hem of the camisole stopping mid thigh. If she bent over, maybe she could pull him from whatever thoughts were keeping him from touching her and being all over her right now.

He pulled off his shirt and tossed it in the laundry basket just inside the bathroom. Emily pulled the clip from the back of her hair and then tossed her head slightly to allow the long dark tresses to drop down past her shoulders. She stepped closer to him as he pulled off his socks and started to undo his belt buckle. She raised her hand and then set it gently on his chest. The dark hair was so inviting to touch, and when she flicked her gaze up to his, he was watching her as if he'd figured out exactly what she was trying to do.

"I need a shower," he muttered, but he didn't pull her hand away or make a move toward the bathroom.

"Do you want me to wash your back?" she said as he skimmed his hand over her cheek. He had that dark, brooding gaze that he got when he was about to take her and have his way with her, but irritation still lurked behind it.

"I may not be gentle tonight, Em," he began, but he said nothing else, as if giving her a moment to understand. Then he held his hand out to her as he stepped inside the bathroom.

She knew he was leaving the ball in her court. Brad was a man who was all fire and passion, but he couldn't hide anything he was feeling from her. When they made love and he was inside her, it was then that she connected with the many overwhelming sides to her man. There was the gentle lover who took his time, teased her, and drove her wild when he was calm and everything in their life was centered. Then there was excited Brad, when their life was a celebration filled with good news. He took her wherever and whenever he could find her alone: over a table, in the barn, even in the forest. Then there was brooding, angry Brad, when someone had pushed him over the edge or when he was upset, hurt, or just plain angry.

That Brad was the one she had now. He wasn't here often, but when he was, he could be rough and fast, taking her over and over until he was so exhausted that he fell asleep while still buried deep inside her. The sex with this Brad was wild and hard, and she had to jam her hand in her mouth when she came, as it was always way hotter, way stronger, and way more powerful than with her other Brads. There were times like now that she craved this

Brad, knowing the sex was going to be wild, frantic, and beyond good.

She put her hand in his and allowed him to pull her into the bathroom, and he closed the door behind them before reaching in and turning on the shower. He watched her as he unzipped his jeans and slid them off along with his briefs. He was already hard for her as she lifted off the silk camisole, tossing it on the floor in a pile with his clothes, stepping into the shower and allowing him to pull the glass door closed behind them. The hot spray was in her face for only a second before he lifted her against the shower wall, her legs wrapped around his waist.

He was kissing her hard, deeply, urgently, and he pressed her arms to the shower wall above her head. He had her exactly where he wanted her, where he needed her. He took both of her wrists in one hand, holding tight so she couldn't move or pull away. He ran his other hand between them and pulled away to bite her lower lip as he moved to bury himself inside her—hard, with a single thrust that knocked the breath out of her. She could feel every inch of him. He lifted one of her legs higher so he could go deeper still, and he pulled out just enough to move back into her, each time forcing a gasp out of her as he slid every inch of himself all the way in, deeply.

She wondered for a moment if he was bigger, as the sheer size of him tonight was taking her breath away. This wasn't making love or just sex: It was him taking her, and there were times that she wanted this pure animal sex, times when he needed her just like this. He pounded into her over and over, and he must have felt the moment she was going to lose it, as he pressed his body against hers, pushing her flat against the wall when she started to come undone. Then he was kissing her again, holding her wrists as she felt herself come completely apart around him. He kept moving in and out. There was nothing soft about him tonight, and he swore right before he came inside her, the warm water soaking them. She stayed right where she was, completely open for her husband, unable to move even if she wanted to. This was just a taste of what she was in for tonight.

$$Chapter\ 10$$

"Happy birthday to you. Happy birthday to you. Happy birthday, dear Trevor …"

Everyone sang. Deep baritones, altos, and sopranos all mixed together as Emily carried a three-layer white chocolate cake to the table. It was ablaze with thirteen green candles: Trevor's favorite color for Trevor's favorite cake. This year, he didn't hide when everyone sang to him. He *was* making a face, though, his lips quirked to the side in an odd smile. He crossed his arms, waiting everyone out.

Everyone was sitting around the large dark oak dining room table in the separate room they used only on special occasions, of which this was one. His grandparents were sitting across the table, Neil was holding Cat on his lap, Candy beside him, and the baby was in the swing, his eyes wide, going back and forth just inside the doorway. Brad put his hand on Emily's lower back as she put the cake in front of Trevor. The girls, Katy and little Becky, were on either side of him. Everyone was clapping and laughing.

"Okay, close your eyes, Trevor. Make a wish," Emily said.

Trevor squeezed his eyes shut and said, "I wish for … hmm."

Brad slid his arm around Emily and pulled her against him, swaying as she fit so easily in his arms. "Not out loud. Say it in your head."

Trevor popped his eyes open, looking up at Brad, and said, "Okay, Dad." He closed his eyes again tightly, and his lips moved. Then he nodded. "Okay, I wished for the Star Wars Encyclopedia."

"Trevor, you're not supposed to tell us! That's not a wish," Katy said.

"But how would you know to get it for me, then?" he said seriously.

"You make a good point, Trevor," Neil said, jabbing his finger at his nephew, and Brad reached down and rustled the top of his son's dark hair.

"What?" Trevor said, smiling in his mischievous way as he glanced up at Brad.

"Okay, who wants cake?" Emily said as she started to lift out the candles. Katy and Becky reached out and quickly grabbed out the others, licking off the icing. There was a knock on the screen door. Brad slid his hand down Emily's backside, and she looked up at him, still feeling the connection with him from last night. He'd taken her again in the shower and three times on the bed before falling asleep. "You expecting anyone?" she asked.

He just shook his head. "No, I'll see who it is. No one start without me! I want the biggest piece," Brad said, and everyone laughed.

He listened to the clink of dishes and lively chatter as he started toward the door, happy that everything for

Trevor's birthday had gone well today. His dad and Neil had chatted and kept things light, everyone was on their best behavior, and he was relieved.

He pulled open the door, still smiling, and took in a woman with her back to the door, a pale knitted hat over her hair. Brad opened the screen door. "Can I help you?" he said.

When she turned around, he felt as if the world tilted for a second. He was staring into the icy blue eyes of Crystal, Trevor's mother.

"Hello, Brad," she said.

"Brad, who is it?"

He heard Emily come up behind him, but it didn't register until he heard her hiss beside him. She touched his arm, and he felt her trembling.

Crystal was standing on the front porch in a black wool coat. "Hello, Emily," she said. Brad noticed she was holding a plastic bag in her hands, and for a moment she appeared uncomfortable, standing there. For the life of him, Brad couldn't figure out why she was here. She had promised never to return, yet here she was, on his doorstep, on the day of his son's birthday.

"What do you want?"

It must have come out quite sharply, as he noticed she blanched before pursing her lips.

"It's Trevor's birthday, and I …" She stopped. Her hand was trembling. She swallowed. "I wanted to give my son a present."

Going through his mind were a hundred things. She couldn't be sincere, so what did she really want? It had been seven years since he paid her off after she signed the divorce papers and signed away her rights as a parent. She'd made her choice then, and it had been about the money. She'd never loved Trevor. Crystal had never under-stood how to be a mother. He could feel Emily digging her nails into his arm, and when he glanced down at her, he saw something on her face that he hadn't seen in a long time: fear.

Chapter 11

Staring at the woman who had turned her life upside down and almost destroyed her and Brad was stirring up that unsettled feeling that had been whispering at Emily's back for the past few days. Was it a premonition she was having, or was it just women's intuition warning her that all good things had to be tested? Having Crystal here was not a test Emily wanted any part of, though. She wanted to scream at the woman, tell her to go away. She could hear the chairs in the dining room scraping back, and she panicked because the last thing she wanted was for the kids to see Crystal here.

"Brad, Trevor …" was all she could get out.

His mouth was tight, and he nodded and then tilted his head toward the dining room. "Go on back inside. I'll be there in a minute."

She knew what he was saying: *Keep the kids in there, especially Trevor. Distract them.* She just didn't want to leave Brad here with this woman, not now, not ever, not for two seconds. She didn't trust her. She was a viper, and, as far as Emily was concerned, she was capable of anything. "Brad

…" she started, not wanting to move, still holding on to his arm.

"Go now," he said brusquely, so unlike him. She knew now wasn't the time to argue, so she nodded. When she glanced over at Crystal, who looked at her and then Brad, she wondered what was going through the woman's head. Emily started back into the dining room, each step an effort. Her legs felt like lead.

Neil was the first one she saw, and he must have picked up on her distress, as he was instantly alert. It was in his face, his eyes.

"Who's at the door, Mom?" Katy asked.

Her throat was dry as she glanced across the table at Brad's parents. Rodney was watching her closely, as well, but it was Neil she looked at. She swallowed the thick lump and said, "No one. Where are we with this cake?"

She tried to sound interested as she stared at the cake she'd spent hours creating for Trevor. All the joy had completely seeped out of this moment. Why did Crystal have to show up now, and why had Brad sent her away so he could talk to his ex-wife alone? She didn't want that woman anywhere near Brad.

She heard a chair scrape back and glanced up at Neil as he plopped Cat in his chair. He looked so good in his burgundy sweater and black jeans, and he touched Candy's bare shoulder as he walked around to Emily. She wondered if he could read minds. This was the Neil she knew, the brother-in-law she loved. He was so astute and caring, an amazing man. He rubbed her arm and said, "Hey, listen, how about you all wait for the cake until I get your dad back here?" When she glanced up at him, he squeezed her shoulder again. "I'll be right back."

Then he left, and she could hear his footsteps as he walked to the door. She heard the screen door squeak open and closed just as another chair scraped back. This time, Rodney stood.

"I'll be right back, as well." He tossed his napkin on the table and started around to the door. "You kids stay in here or there'll be no cake for any of you," he said teasingly.

"Ah, Grandpa, how long do we have to wait?" the kids all whined. Trevor stuck his finger in the icing and shoved a glob into his mouth.

"Mmm, good," he said, grinning up at Emily.

Emily was so flustered that she bumped Katy's glass of sparkling juice, spilling the purple liquid all over the white tablecloth.

"Oh, Mom!" Katy shrieked.

Brad's mother scooted back her chair. "I'll get a cloth," she said. Rodney touched Emily's shoulder, and she didn't miss his frown—of course he could see how upset she was. Then he, too, left and went to the door. What she would have given in that moment to be a fly on the wall, to know exactly what was going on. At least Brad wasn't alone with Crystal, and knowing Rodney and Neil were there gave her some comfort.

There was concern in Candy's expression as she watched Emily from across the table. "Everything okay?" she said.

Emily tried to say it would be, but she couldn't get the words out of her mouth.

Chapter 12

B rad did not want Crystal anywhere near his children. In fact, he didn't want her on this property or in this state, for that matter. He had to remind himself they were divorced, she had signed away her parental rights, and she had no hold here anymore. She was powerless, so why did he feel as if he was missing a really big piece of the puzzle? With Crystal, anything was possible, and to dismiss her and turn his back on her was a mistake he didn't ever want to make again.

He heard the door open behind him and only glanced to the side when he realized Neil was beside him. "Crystal" was all his brother said, standing beside him and crossing his arms.

"You look good, Neil." She seemed flustered and gave him an awkward smile, which was so unlike Crystal, who was the epitome of calm, cool, and calculating.

"Brad, you've got kids who—" Rodney stopped talking as he stepped out, holding the door open. Brad turned to his dad and saw the emotion flicker across his face. Was he remembering how Crystal had been the source of their estrangement for so many years? Then Rodney stepped outside, letting the door slap closed.

"Rodney, wow, this is awkward." Crystal sighed and looked back at Brad. She was gripping the plastic bag in both hands now. "How's Trevor?" she finally asked.

"Trevor is fine, Crystal. So, again, why are you here? You agreed to stay away. You signed away your rights to him. You promised to never return." Brad was squeezing his fists so hard the tips of his short nails were digging into his rough palms, but he welcomed the discomfort, as it kept him on edge. That was where he needed to be, with Crystal.

She actually flushed. "I did agree to that, but he's still my son, and whether you believe it or not, there isn't a day that has passed that I haven't thought about Trevor and how he's doing." She held out the plastic bag. "I bought this for him."

When Brad didn't move to take the gift, Neil reached out and took it. "Crystal, you should leave. It isn't appropriate for you to be here," he said.

"Could I see him, please, just for a minute? You don't have to tell him who I am. I just need to see him to know he's okay and what he looks like. He's thirteen today."

"It's amazing that after all these years, you decide now to have motherly instincts, to show up here. What do you really want, Crystal?" Brad said.

Rodney touched his arm to get his attention. "You need to get back in there."

Brad just nodded. He noticed the small, compact car parked in front, a black Volkswagen, not something he could ever have pictured Crystal driving.

"I've done a lot of things I regret, and I'm not asking for you to believe I've changed. All I can tell you is that I love my son, and I just want to know how he is. Please, Brad."

The door squeaked, and tears flooded Crystal's wide eyes. Brad jerked around to see his kids staring.

"Trevor, Katy, Becky, get back in here!" Emily called from inside the house.

"Who's here, Dad?" Trevor asked. This was not good, and then Emily was there, and she paled.

"Come back inside and let your dad finish up," she said quickly. "You know better than to interrupt."

He heard a sniff and turned back to Crystal, who had tears running down her face. She sucked her lower lip between her teeth as if she was trying to get herself together. "Was that Trevor?" Her voice caught, and she wiped at her eyes. That was when he noticed she wasn't decked out with her face all made up. She didn't have any eye makeup on at all, which was unusual for Crystal. There was something different about her, but he really didn't want to look too hard. He didn't want her in his life at all.

"Yeah, that was Trevor."

She pressed her lips together to stop the tremble and tried to offer a smile. "He looks good. Oh my God, and he's talking. Were those your other kids?"

"Yeah, Katy's from Emily's first marriage, and little Becky, who we named after Mom, is our youngest."

Crystal gestured to the bag Neil was holding. "It's a Lego mug. I thought he would like it." She sniffed and then pursed her lips, looking away awkwardly. "I hope he likes it. I tried to find something that would interest him, and I saw that, and I just hope, well …" She started to turn away, her hands shoved in her pockets. She looked so pathetic, so lost.

"You can say hi to him, but then you have to go," Brad said.

Neil cleared his throat beside him and leaned closer. "You think that's a good idea?"

"Could I?" She stepped back toward him and actually started to reach out to touch him, but she must have thought better of it, as she lowered her hand to her side.

His dad put his hand on his shoulder. Maybe it was a warning that he shouldn't have offered, but there was something about her standing here that, for a moment, made things seem not so black and white. Maybe he shouldn't have said it. He hadn't thought it through clearly. "I'm serious, Crystal, no bullshit. You say hi, and then you leave."

She nodded to him, and he didn't miss the heavy sigh of disapproval from Neil.

Brad just wanted her gone. At the same time, he was feeling guilty—for what, he didn't have a clue. This woman had turned his life upset down, messed with his head, his heart, and his feelings, and lied and cheated on him—and here he was, opening the door and letting her back in his house.

She stepped inside. She was wearing flat black shoes, and she looked around.

Neil grabbed his arm, pulling him back, his dad on his other side. "I hope you know what you're doing, Brad. Don't you remember what she did? That woman was always trouble."

Brad pulled his arm away. "I just want her gone."

"Gone, really? So why'd you just invite her in?"

He pulled his arm away. He couldn't help being angry with Neil—or rather still angry, as nothing had changed from yesterday with his brother.

They followed her inside, and it was Emily he saw first across the room: her eyes wide, her lips tight, her arms around the children. It was the look of a hurt and confused woman he hadn't seen in a long time. He wanted to kick himself for putting that uncertainty there now.

"Trevor, this woman wants to say hi to you. She brought you a present for your birthday." Brad was curt, direct.

"Who are you?" Trevor asked.

Crystal glanced awkwardly at Brad and said, as she took another step closer, "I'm your mother."

Chapter 13

She scrubbed at the cake pan over and over with the scouring pad, then felt a hand touch her arm.

"I think you're wearing off the enamel. You can stop scrubbing. That spot isn't going to get any cleaner." Candy reached for the dish towel and held out her hand for the pan.

Emily leaned against the sink on her elbows, resting her hands over the sudsy water, dropping her head in defeat. She felt as if she'd been running on a treadmill and had finally stopped, and her head was starting to ache. Maybe Candy knew, as she rubbed her back and then her shoulders. She didn't say a word. What could she say to anyone after this birthday fiasco?

"Is she gone?" Emily asked. She hoped she was, as she was shell shocked, unable to believe Crystal had been in her house, a house Crystal had first shared with Brad. For a moment, she felt herself thrown back to that day when she'd first worked here for Brad and Crystal had returned, walking in with her suitcases and saying she was home to stay. It had been horrible, awful, the hell she'd walked through just to get to this point. Trevor was *her* son. That woman had abandoned him and done nothing to help him. Emily had worked with him, loved him, taught him, fought his battles for him, with Brad by her side.

"Yeah, she's still here," Candy said.

"Candy, the baby's awake." Neil was in the doorway, and Emily glanced up from where she was leaning pathetically over the sink. Her eyes burned, and she thought she was going to be sick for a moment. Neil could be such a strong support, she realized. He was watching her with compassion and a strength she wanted to lean on.

Candy rubbed her back again. "You're going to be okay. Just remember you're his mother. Trevor would be nowhere without you," she said. She stopped beside Neil on her way out, and he rubbed his hand over her bare arm. She touched his face. With Candy's newfound confidence and Neil's strength, a powerful and strong love had grown between them. At this moment, Emily envied them.

The way Neil watched her, his wife, as she walked away, there was no doubt of the depth of his love for her. Then she was gone, and Neil glanced into the living room, where everyone was except her. Emily was hiding out here in the kitchen. She couldn't be in the same room with that woman. Neil moved into the kitchen and stood beside her, then leaned down as well so they were eye level, side by side.

He nudged her playfully. "A penny for your thoughts, Em?"

She wanted to cry, and she choked out a pathetic half laugh, half sob as Neil pulled her into his arms and hugged her, rubbing her back. He had such strong arms.

"It's going to be okay. Sometimes situations look about as bad as can be, but they never are."

She wondered if he really believed that or if he was

saying it for her benefit. "Why did he let her in, Neil? My husband brought that woman into our house. He never even asked me," she said, and she could tell when she pulled away and rubbed her eyes, struggling to hold it together, that Neil wasn't happy about the situation, either.

"Yeah, I don't know why my brother let her come in. Crystal always was able to sway him when the rest of us could see through her."

Did Neil have any idea that was exactly what she didn't want to hear? It was a fear she still carried, though she hadn't realized it until now. Yes, they'd walked through hell to find a way to each other, even though Crystal and Emily's ex had been pulling at each of them with their hooks, trying to tear them apart. She'd wondered then if it would ever be possible for them to be together, but they'd crawled over that mountain to reach each other, and now, after all these years, this woman had walked right back into their lives.

"I don't want her here, Neil. Brad should've asked me. I'm Trevor's mother. This is his birthday. I'm the one who's been there for him, done everything for him"—she jabbed her hand toward the living room—"yet she's in there with him, and I feel as if I've been banned to the kitchen as the hired help." She tried to keep her voice down, wondering if anyone had heard her. She felt dampness on her cheek, and Neil, who was watching her with such understanding, reached down and wiped away the tear.

"You are his mother," he said. "A mother isn't who gives birth to a child, Emily. You know that. A mother is the woman who loves the child, who holds him every night when he cries, who comforts him, teaches him, dresses him, and loves him enough to see that he has everything he needs. That's you, and without you, where would Trevor be? My brother …" He just shook his head. "Brad loves you so much, and it's you who's filled my brother's life with the kind of happiness he never had before, not Crystal, so don't let this fuck with your head."

She'd never heard Neil speak like that. Behind them, someone cleared his throat, and Emily jumped.

Brad was standing in the archway behind her, his expression weary. He glanced over at Neil, who had his hand on her shoulder. "Crystal is leaving," he said.

Emily couldn't say anything. She just nodded. Brad stood there, looking down at her, and, for the life of her, she couldn't figure out what was going through his head. This was the first time she could ever remember wanting to hit him on his arms, his chest—just wail on him. She couldn't, though. She wasn't a violent person.

Once again, he'd hurt her with his distance, but instead of stepping into the kitchen and apologizing and holding her, which she willed him to do, he just shook his head as she stared at him with anger, hurt, resentment—everything she wanted to hurl his way. He walked off, and Emily picked up the scrubber in the sink and attacked another pot.

Chapter 14

Brad watched as Crystal drove away. He was alone on the porch, and the sun was setting at the edge of the tree line on this clear evening. He needed a minute to gather his thoughts and come to some kind understanding about what had just happened before stepping back into the house to face everyone. His mother hadn't tried to hide her disapproval, Neil was furious and had shaken his head, as if he needed to reinforce what an idiot he thought Brad was, and his father, Rodney, hadn't said a word. He had just watched Crystal from across the room, and not once had his gaze met Brad's.

Maybe Rodney was reliving the rift that had torn apart their relationship. They hadn't spoken for all those years, all because his father had tried to warn him about Crystal, the woman she was. Brad had lashed out as an angry, self-centered young man, saying things to his father that he still wished he could go back in time and undo. But there were no do overs in life. You had to live with all the ugliness you created, the hurt you caused, and the bad you were responsible for.

The look on Emily's face, as she'd stood with their three children, now haunted him. He'd never seen her so pale, and by the uncertainty in her eyes, he knew she was scared. He wanted to kick himself, knowing he was responsible for the heartache on the face of the woman he loved. Emily hadn't said a word when Crystal told Trevor she was his mother, but she had flinched, and her heartache was apparent as she stood stiffly. Brad had wiped his face and taken in the shocked expression on little Becky's face as she looked up at Trevor and then over to the strange woman. She was the only one who'd had no idea that Emily wasn't Trevor's real mother.

Damn it to hell! Brad wanted to kick himself. He couldn't believe how badly he'd screwed that up. Where the security and wellbeing of his children and family were concerned, he didn't make mistakes—yet he had.

The door clattered, and he didn't glance around to see who was there. His father cleared his throat as he came up beside him. "Not what you were expecting for a family birthday," he said, sounding calm.

Brad couldn't answer. He was torn on how to deal with this revelation with Trevor. For some reason that Brad still couldn't make sense of, Trevor understood who Crystal was. He had been the only one in the room who'd stepped toward her, seeming happy to see her. He'd held out his hand and said, "You're my mom." Brad couldn't figure out how he could know that, understand that, and not be upset with the situation.

Trevor had been only a baby when Crystal walked out, and he had been three when she returned for a short time, but he never spoke of her, ever. Then again, Trevor didn't understand or see things the same way others did. It wasn't so black and white for him—or even a murky shade of gray. He didn't get stuck in the past. He was always in the moment, in the present. He didn't seem to hold on to hurts or judgments, and his perception of things was different, too. He was happy, and to him, Crystal's visit was something extra to make his birthday special.

Crystal had sat on the sofa, Trevor directly across from her, Katy beside him, and everyone but Emily had stood at a different spot in the living room and watched. Emily had quietly slipped away to the kitchen. He should have gone after her, but he couldn't leave Trevor with Crystal. Even though his parents and Neil were in the living room, watching, he felt he needed to stay and somehow control the situation. He was worried about a lot of things, including what else Crystal would say to his son.

She'd grinned for the longest time before gesturing to the bag Neil still held. "I brought you a present."

Trevor, of course, had been ecstatic, standing up and saying, "A present? Where is it?"

Neil held the bag out, and Trevor took it, pulling out a wrapped box. He ripped off the paper and opened the gift, and his eyes lit up. A Lego mug! He started snapping the Lego pieces onto it. "Thank you," he said, but he didn't look her way, engrossed with it. He was so happy. "Katy, look!"

He always shared everything with Katy, and she glanced nervously over at Brad and then said, "That's nice."

What Brad was having a hard time with was that Trevor didn't seem to carry any hard feelings toward Crystal. A typical child would be angry with his mother for abandoning him, would be curious, too, and maybe quiet, unsure. But Trevor was just happy, and he sat beside her on the sofa after assembling what he said was a robot. She touched his hand, and he let her. She asked him questions, but he didn't understand half of them, as they were too abstract. He'd say "Good" or "Fine" or ask her, "Do you like Lego Star Wars?"

She looked to Brad a couple times for help, but he just stood there. It was Becky who finally stepped into the middle of the room, clapped her hands together, and said, "Well, this has been fun, but Crystal only stopped by for a minute, and she has to go now."

It was what he should have done. She'd overstayed her welcome, overstepped her boundaries. He felt as if he'd dropped the ball. Now, as he stood on the front porch with his dad, he was bothered by what Trevor had said to her at the door before she left: "Come back again." He had waved, holding up his mug.

He prayed she wouldn't, as he shook his head, and he knew she understood his meaning, but there was something in the way she looked at Trevor and then avoided Brad that made him realize he'd just cracked open a can of worms that couldn't be closed again.

"You need to talk to your wife," Rodney said, squeezing his shoulder. "Brad, go in there and be with her."

He took a deep breath. "I hurt her."

His dad didn't say a word for the longest time. "What's done is done, Brad. She showed up here, put you on the spot." He took a breath as if deciding not to say anymore.

"And what would you have done, Dad, if you were me?" Brad crossed his arms, feeling the chill in the air. His shirt was thin and fine for inside, but it was getting cold outside in the evenings now. He should get his coat, check on the animals, but he had a family to face—his children, and Emily.

"I don't know, Brad, honestly. It's a fine mess, and that woman turned your life upside down. I have no use for her, and she never gave Trevor a second thought. He didn't fit into her lifestyle, you know that, but why would she come back here after all these years? What does she really want, money?" His dad was shaking his head. "She wants something, Brad, and you should be worried. I'm dumbfounded as to why she showed up, but there's something about her that scares me. If she comes back, I'd send her away if I were you."

It was the first time he realized that his dad wasn't just worried about what Crystal would do but about the strain she could cause in this family. "I guess I better go and talk to Emily," Brad said.

His dad glanced toward the door. "I think your mother is with her in the kitchen, and your brother, too. The kids put aside a piece of cake for you."

Brad walked inside and found the kids in the living room. There were plates of half-eaten cake on the coffee table, and Katy was coloring with Cat. Crayons covered the living room coffee table.

Little Becky raced over to him. "Daddy, is she gone?"

He lifted her up and kissed her plump cheek. "Yeah, honey."

"Daddy, why did she say she's Trevor's mother? Isn't Mom?"

He closed his eyes. He'd confused his daughter. This was something that was never talked about, not in this house. "Your mom is Trevor's mother. Let's be clear on that." He noticed then that Neil had stepped into the living room and lifted Cat in his arms, kissing her cheek, and she smiled.

Neil gestured to the kitchen. "Your wife is in with Mom. Why don't I take the kids up and get them ready for bed? Becky and Cat, anyway."

"Katy, you and Trevor head up, too," Brad said as he

started to put Becky down, but she held on, and he could tell she was scared.

"Daddy, is a woman going to show up here for me, too, and say she's my mother? Is that lady going to come back and take Trevor?" Her tiny hands were wrapped around his neck, and he held her, his six-year-old daughter. He wanted to kick his own ass even more for the fear he'd put into his little girl. He kissed her cheek and held her tight, rubbing her back. Then Emily was in the archway, all mama bear, ready to lay into him.

"Look, all of you. This is your mom," Brad said. He walked over to Emily, who made no move to take one step closer to him, and his mother slid her arm around Emily's shoulder and raised an eyebrow at him. He could tell that Emily was considering moving away, but she looked at Becky in his arms and must have seen how upset she was. Emily stood stiffly beside him, and he knew that she was staying where she was only because of their children. Oh, boy, was he in trouble. He wondered what kind of groveling and begging and penance he was going to have to do to dig himself out of this mess. Couldn't she understand his dilemma? This was a marriage, and he needed her to back him, no questions asked. "No one is coming in here and taking anyone. Crystal may have given birth to Trevor, but she's not his mother—and, Becky, I can guarantee your mother struggled for hours, giving birth to you. I was there. You're ours, too."

Everyone was staring at Brad, and no one seemed happy at all, but Trevor held up his Lego mug and said, "Okay, Dad. Is my mom coming back again tomorrow?"

Emily gasped, and Neil shut his eyes and shook his head.

Becky seemed to know this was only going in one direction—from bad to worse. She clapped her hands again.

"Okay, kids, upstairs. Trevor, Katy, brush your teeth after all that cake."

"Brad, I'll take your little miss Becky up with me and toss her in the bath with Cat," Neil said, trying to lighten the mood or maybe distract the kids and break the tension filling the air.

Brad set his daughter down, and his mom went up the stairs behind Trevor and Katy, Neil with the two girls. Candy was standing at the foot of the stairs with the baby, and Rodney was beside her. It was awkward, as Emily had now stepped out of his arms.

"You know what? I'm going to check on the cattle, the horses, see that your hands took care of everything for the night," Rodney announced. He opened the closet door and pulled out his coat.

Candy cleared her throat and said, "I'm going to go help Neil," and she started up the stairs with the baby.

"You know what? I'm tired. I'm going to have a bath and read," Emily said, looking at her hands—anywhere but at Brad. She started to walk past him.

His hand shot out, gripping her arm to stop her. "Em, don't do this."

"Don't do what, Brad? Have a bath and walk away? Or maybe you need to pull the rug out from under me again."

This time, when she looked at him, the fury burning in her deep blue eyes was beyond anything he'd ever seen before. "I'm sorry, Em. Please don't walk away. Please just stay and talk to me."

When he reached to touch her cheek, expecting her to lean in as she always did and soften from his touch, she did something she'd never done before: She stepped back one step, two steps, and turned her head away.

Chapter 15

There was no one left downstairs, no one she could use as an excuse to avoid this confrontation with Brad—all six feet of hard muscle before her now. She was so mad and hurt and disillusioned … yet she loved him, and that was what made the hurt so much worse. How could he have treated her as if she didn't matter? Even though she knew that wasn't exactly the truth of the situation, her heart hadn't gotten that message. When she tried to step around him, he took another step and blocked her way, then another until he was right in front of her and she couldn't slip past him.

"Em, please." The softness in his voice brought the sting of tears to her eyes. She could hear how bad he felt.

"Brad, I love you, but you brought her into our house—on Trevor's birthday, no less. Do you have any idea how you made me feel? I felt dismissed, and I was reliving the nightmare of when she first showed up here. Do you remember when I first came to work here and there was you and me, and then Crystal came back? She nearly destroyed me, Brad, with the games and the disrespect and the stress. It nearly destroyed us. You remember all the lies she told, her deception, what she did with Trevor, yet you allowed her to walk back in here tonight."

He was staring at her, his expression filled with emotion: deep, remorseful, and upset, whether for him or her she didn't know. "I'm sorry, Em. It caught me off guard. I never expected her to show up here again. She seemed different, and she never showed any interest in Trevor before, but here she was on his birthday, remembering, and she just wanted to see him. I don't know why I said yes, but I did. I can't undo it even if I wanted to."

He put his hands on her shoulders. She loved it when he touched her, but right now she was so mad and hurt that any touch of his was like gasoline on a fire. She tried to push his arms away.

"Stop fighting me, Em. This is me. I love you."

"I know that!" she shouted.

He dropped his arms. "What is it, then? She's gone. Can't you just let it go?"

She couldn't believe he was that dense. Brad Friessen wasn't a stupid man. He frustrated her at times, was overbearing, strong, and opinionated, but she believed he'd always had her back—until today. Didn't he understand that he had let a viper into their home?

"Brad, we never told Trevor or Becky about Crystal," she said. "We kind of just ignored it, ignored her. She went away, and we were happy about that. We have our family. Trevor's made incredible progress, but what you did, in a matter of a few thoughtless moments, was bring a whole bunch of uncertainty into his life. He doesn't understand things as you and I do. Nothing is black and white for him, and there's no abstract, either, Brad. She wasn't even in his head, not even a thought, until now. What have you done? I don't think you have any idea what's in store for us, what you've just now brought back into our lives."

"Em, she wanted to see him. I don't think it's as bad as you're making it out to be. You're being too dramatic, creating a problem that isn't there. Just let it go, Em."

She hated it when he talked like this, as if she was the one making something out of nothing. It was just like a man to think that if you ignored a problem, it would go away. "Let it go? You know what? I'm going to bed. You deal with the kids and this mess you've created."

He wouldn't move. He was right in front of her, looking down at her. He let out a weary sigh as if she was causing him all manner of grief. "I'm here trying to clear the air with you, apologizing to you, and you want to run away?"

She couldn't believe him. "Are you kidding me? That wasn't much of an apology. You just told me I'm making too much out of you bringing that leper into this house. You saw your daughter, how upset she was. She's afraid Crystal is going to come in here and take Trevor. Maybe this was a talk we should've had with the kids, telling them exactly where things stand and how I fit into Trevor's life."

He put his hands on her shoulders again and rubbed even when she tried to move away. "Hey, stop it, would you? I screwed up, okay? Is that what you want to hear? God, everyone here knows it: my brother, my father, my mother ... I'm sorry, Em. The last thing I ever want to do is scare our kids. You know I would walk through fire for all of you. I don't want this to come between us. She's gone. She saw him, and she won't be back. The kids have nothing to worry about."

Was he trying to placate her? "You're a fool if you believe that, Brad. You remember what she did. She lies, and it has absolutely nothing to do with love. It was about her not giving up what she believed was hers, even though Trevor and you didn't fit her lifestyle. Her act here …" She shook her head. She still couldn't believe it was the same Crystal she had once known who walked into this house and sat on the sofa, looking awkward, no longer dressed like a fashion model. No, this Crystal was average, driving an average car—but there was one thing Emily knew deep in her bones. With Crystal, there was never anything simple, anything average, and she was anything but easy. No, that woman wanted something. There was no one who could convince her that the woman's interest had anything to do with Trevor, a boy with autism, a boy who needed so much care, so much help and attention, who still had mountains to climb.

"You never asked me what I thought, Brad. You never asked me if it was okay for her to see Trevor, to come into our home and disrupt his birthday party, and that hurts me most of all."

He ran his hands up and over her cheeks and into her hair, holding her still. "I'm so sorry," he said.

"But you'd do it again, wouldn't you?" She was so hurt and mad that she just couldn't let him off the hook.

He didn't say anything, and this time, when she pulled away and walked around him, he let her walk away.

Chapter 16

Brad slid the stall door closed in the barn. The overhead lights were burning bright against the black of night. The house was quiet, and he could tell from where he stood in the barn, staring at the house in the distance with only a few lights on, that the kids were in bed and everyone else was settling in for the night.

"Hey."

He glanced over to his brother, who was standing just inside the barn, holding two steaming mugs.

He held one of the mugs out to Brad. "Irish coffee, with lots of Irish. Thought you could use it."

Neil still hadn't shaved, and Brad would have normally asked, but right about now it wasn't really important. He was in a black coat and jeans, his boots scraping as he stepped over to Brad.

Brad hung the rake on the hook and took the mug from Neil. He could smell the Irish whiskey before it came close to his lips. The burn was welcome, and the bite of alcohol was what he needed. "Thank you."

Neil didn't say anything as he drank his coffee and

looked back at the house. "Do you want to hear what I have to say?"

He couldn't believe his brother was actually asking. "If I say no, are you going to tell me anyway?"

Neil just watched him. "I'm the last person to tell you about the fucking mess you made in there. You know it. But, shit, Brad, what the hell is it with Crystal that you let her walk all over you? She has a way of getting you to soften to her way of thinking. I don't understand why you don't see it, when we all saw what she did to you."

"You're right, Neil, you're the last person who should be giving me any advice, considering the mess you made in your own life."

"There's one thing, though, Brad. It's easier when you're standing on the other side, watching someone else make the mistakes you just finished making. Why do you suppose Crystal is here?" Neil sat down on a bale of hay, holding the mug.

"I don't know. I don't understand her. I never did." Brad hadn't thought of Crystal in so long. There were times here and there that she passed through his mind: an expression on Trevor's face that resembled her, or a gesture he made that was so similar to hers that it could have been her in front of him. Then he'd see Emily, his wife, who was everything to him and showed him what real, unconditional deep love was. He'd never felt what he had with Emily with Crystal. Standing here in the night, reliving the hurt he'd put on his wife's face on a day that was so special, made him feel like a fool. It should have been just them, and he couldn't help wishing he could go back to that moment and turn Crystal away from the door. Could he have done that? He should have. He wished she'd never knocked on his door to begin with.

"I just hope she doesn't come back," Brad said. "I've

got a lot to make up to my wife to get back in her good books You know what Crystal did to her before, with the games. She hurt Emily so badly. Today, watching my wife, I felt like a fumbling fool. I didn't know what to do, Neil, and Mom had to step in and tell her it was time to go when I should have. That was my responsibility."

"You need to be careful, Brad. You told her once to say hi then leave, nothing else. She walked in the door and told him she was his mother. *Emily* is his mother. Ask yourself, is Trevor going to be confused now? What will this do to the relationship between Trevor and Emily? I'm not here every day to see how Trevor reacts. You are." Neil leaned back against the barn wall.

"All of Trevor's progress is Emily, you know that. I don't have to tell you."

Neil nodded. Of course he knew.

"Did you see Crystal, the average car she was driving, no makeup, and her clothes? There was nothing flashy about her today."

His brother took another swallow of coffee, his deep brown eyes watching Brad over the rim of his cup.

"Do you suppose, after all these years, she really has been thinking about Trevor, and today really was about seeing how he was? Maybe she's suddenly thinking of him?"

"I think you need to ask yourself, Brad, if you and your family can afford to take that chance. Your situation isn't that different from mine. If Maria showed up and wanted to see the baby …" He shook his head, and the darkness that appeared in his expression made Brad wonder what he'd do to the woman. There was nothing friendly in his face, in his eyes. "I hurt Candy by bringing Maria into my life without taking into consideration how it would all play out and how my wife would be affected. I take more care in my business deals. What does that say about me? I almost broke her spirit, and never again will I allow something like that to happen. I love her too much. This is my family. Dad was right about one thing: I made a promise to my wife, and I'm damn sure going to keep it."

"Are you going to tell your wife the truth, Neil, about Michael? I've got to tell you, the truth has a way of coming out when you least want it to. Secrets and lies, they don't work. It would be better if you came clean—"

"And deal with the fallout." Neil cut him off. "Is that what you're going to say?" He had that unreasonable attitude again. "No." He stood up, brushing the hay from his jeans. "I have my wife back, and I'm not messing with that and taking a chance on losing her. No way in hell. I may be a fool, but this secret is one that will never be told."

"What secret?"

Brad never heard his dad approach. He had to be slipping. Neil was looking pretty tight lipped. Rodney Friessen glanced from Brad to Neil and then back again to Neil, waiting for someone to tell him. "Was wondering where you two were. Your mother sent me out to talk some sense into Brad. Neil, we need to have a talk anyway, so maybe it's best that you're both here."

"Dad, look …" Neil started with that cocky attitude, and Brad said nothing, just watched. Neil and his dad used to be close, but between them now was indifference, mistrust, and awkwardness. It was almost the same as the rift that had existed between him and his dad when Crystal was in the picture.

"No, you look, Neil. I never said anything to you. You up and left the estate, going after your wife and moving her away, which was the right thing to do. Your mother wanted me to call you half a dozen times in Arizona over that Maria thing. We didn't know what happened, and I'm not getting in your business, but your mom has noticed. Did you think you could hide it? Little Michael looks just like you did when you were a baby."

Brad could see the distress Neil was doing his best to hide.

"You said Maria lost the baby, but here you have a little boy who would be the same age," Rodney said. "If your mom figured it out, how long do you think it's going to be before your wife does?"

Brad could see Neil thinking as he wiped his face with his hand. "Dad's right, Neil. Candy's going to wonder soon. Women are smart, and if Mom figured it out, Candy will, too. I told you it would be better coming from you."

Neil went quiet, deep in thought. He was battling something, but he would never share it. Brad supposed his brother was just like him, needing to work it through in his own mind and come to terms with it first.

"And, Brad, Crystal showing up here the way she did … you've got to make sure she stays away from your boy, from your family," Rodney said. "Whatever's going on, you can't trust her. She's up to something. She wants something. You have to know that."

Instead of clearing the air, this little talk seemed to heighten the tension between his dad, Neil, and him.

Maybe his dad knew, as he gestured with his hand while taking in both Brad and Neil. "Look, you two, you're not kids anymore, and we all make mistakes. Hell, I'm no saint, and if your mother wasn't a forgiving woman, she'd have left me years ago. But she didn't. She stayed, and we worked things out between us, which is what you do with the woman you love. Brad, you've got a sweet woman inside with a broken heart. And, Neil, you have to do right by Candy, because the kind of secrets you're keeping are the kind that will tear a marriage apart." Rodney watched

Neil for the longest time and then shook his head, starting to turn away.

"Dad," Brad called out as his strong, tall, gray-haired father, a man he respected, turned back around and faced him. "Thank you."

A hint of humor touched his dad's lips, maybe a smile. Then he turned and started back to the house.

"Well, Neil, Dad's right about one thing. I have a sweet wife who's madder than hell at me, and I need to go make it right." Brad looped his arm around Neil's shoulder. "Come on, let's go. Don't be so mad, because Dad's right about a lot of things, Neil."

His brother only grunted as Brad flicked off the light and pulled the barn door closed, and they headed back to the dimly lit, quiet house.

Chapter 17

S he could hear the sounds of a house being locked up for the night. Rodney and Becky had already gone to bed. She'd heard Candy with the baby, settling him in for the night, as well. Brad and Neil were still downstairs. She had the bedside light on as she tried to read a book by one of her favorite authors, who always pulled her into a story, but not tonight. She'd read the same page over and over and still didn't have a clue what was happening.

She'd already soaked in the bath, letting Brad deal with the kids while she had her very own little pity party. No one had bothered her, but personal space wasn't all it was cracked up to be. She'd cried alone, undisturbed, in the bathtub, hurt over what Brad had done. Now she just felt empty.

The stairs creaked, and for a minute she considered reaching over and shutting off the light, pretending she was asleep. That was below her, something she couldn't do even though she wanted nothing more than to roll over and give Brad the cold shoulder. The problem was that she wanted him to make an effort, and she wanted him to suffer just a bit for what he'd put her through.

She couldn't stop herself from glancing up when the door opened and Brad stepped inside. He closed the door, and for a moment all they did was look at one another from across the room. She swallowed the thick lump in her throat and waited. He pushed away from the door, unbuttoning his shirt and sitting on the bed, the mattress sinking from his weight.

"I'm sorry, Em." He had his back to her and then slid around to face her, resting his large hand over her legs, which were tucked under the covers. "Are you going to give me the cold shoulder all night?"

"Brad …" she started. She had to clear her throat.

He slid closer to her, putting his hand on either side of her, leaning into her space. Her hand ached to reach out and touch him, so much so that she had to squeeze her fist and fight against what her heart wanted and her head told her. Maybe he knew, as he angled his head closer, really looking deeply into her eyes.

"Em, being mad at me and putting up walls isn't going to make this better. I'm sorry you have to forgive me, you have no choice. You know that, don't you?"

She closed up her book and put it down. Brad reached out, taking it from her hands and tossing it to the foot of the bed. "Hey, I was reading that!"

"Really?"

Sometimes it was irritating that he knew her so well. He had a hint of cockiness as he looked at her again. His eyes were powerful, and there was so much to him. He had to know he was wearing her down.

"Brad, I'm so mad at you for letting her come into this house."

"I know, and I'm sorry." He spoke softly, deeply.

"You didn't ask me." She didn't want to cry again. She wasn't a crier, but after he let that woman in, she felt as if all she'd worked for and built with Brad was now threatened.

"It wasn't fair of me to do that."

"She told Trevor she was his mother."

He shut his eyes as if trying to rid himself of a bad memory and shook his head. "It would have come out eventually, Em. It wasn't as if we were keeping it a secret. You're his mother. She may have given birth to him, but that doesn't make her his mother. Everyone knows that, Em."

"Did you see Trevor's reaction? He wasn't angry. He's curious. He's interested in her. She's going to come back, Brad."

He was shaking his head. "No, she won't. I told her not to. She won't be welcome."

"Brad, I don't understand how you could have let her in. Even your brother said she'd always been able to get to you when she couldn't get to anyone else. I remember what she did before, the lengths she went to, the lies. Don't you remember? She tried to destroy me, us. She drove a wedge in between us. I can't go through that again."

"Hey, she's not coming back. In case you've forgotten, you're my wife. She has no hold here anymore. She's out of our lives. I will never allow her or anyone to come into our lives and try to fuck with us, Em. Neil was way off base." Brad leaned back, and he seemed to pull into himself a bit. "I think my brother is reading his own situation into this."

Of course—Neil and Candy. Emily had forgotten. "You found out what's going on with him?"

Brad moved off the bed and pulled off his shirt. "I did."

She waited for him to say something, to tell her what was going on as he dumped his shirt in the laundry hamper. "And?"

He pulled off his socks, and when he glanced over at her, she could see his hesitation about something.

"Brad, what is it?"

He shook his head. "You need to let it go. Right now, I wish I didn't know. I don't have secrets from you, Em, but this isn't my secret." He started toward the bed, and his eyes held anguish and worry right to the depth of his soul.

"Did he kill someone?"

He actually chuckled, then groaned. "I wish. Honestly, Emily, for a moment I thought that, too, but no."

"Then what is it?" She watched him, imploring him to tell her as he rested his arm against the wall, staring out into nothing.

Then he said, "The baby's his, and Candy doesn't know."

Chapter 18

The soft hand running over his chest stirred him from his sleep. He felt her lips press into his stomach and her hand brushing over his hip and lower. He rolled over, trapping her underneath him and settling between her legs.

"Good morning," he whispered as he entered her and then rolled again onto his back, taking her with him so she was astride him. The early morning light was only a flicker in the room. It was still dim, but he could see enough of the curves and silk and satin of her nightgown. He lifted it over her waist and higher, taking the hem and tossing it aside.

She was a beautiful woman, all curves and a generous handful of breasts that he loved to tease and play with while she rode him. She ran her hands through and over his chest hair. He loved listening to her, the sounds she'd make, the tiny gasp when he touched her in that certain way—and right before she'd come. She was so responsive to him as she rose up and down, and he gripped her hips to slow her and hold her, moving her at his speed, his rhythm. When she cried out, he rolled her over again until he had her under him, and he drove into her harder, faster, her hands on his face. She whimpered again, and he let himself go. He didn't know how long he lay there on top of her, still inside her warmth, feeling her hands on his back, his head on her breasts.

"How could Neil do that to Candy, Brad?"

He pulled out of her and rolled over, resting his head on his pillow, his forearm over his eyes. "Oh, why did I tell you?"

She rolled over and rested her hand on his chest. "Brad, that's not fair. I'm your wife. I can't believe you wouldn't share it."

He lifted his arm, taking in Emily's deep blue eyes, the lingering passion that was now fading to a determination he recognized well. "Look, you can't say anything. This is Neil's fuckup, and if you say something to Candy, you could destroy their marriage." He ripped back the covers and put his feet on the icy cold floor.

"That's not fair, Brad. You mustn't think much of me if you believe I would run to Candy and tell her."

Brad didn't turn around, but he could feel the icy glare of his wife. "Look, just drop it. Neil has to figure this out himself. He's dug himself into a hole that only he can fix. I just hope he comes clean to her, because if he doesn't, this kind of thing does have a way of coming out, and after what they've been through …" He had to stop. He loved his brother, but the relationship he had with Candy had been stormy from the beginning. Now, what they had together was good—except it was built on a lie.

"I know, Brad. I've seen how happy Candy is now, but you have to talk to your brother. You have to make him see reason. He has to tell her. I love your family, and Neil is a great guy. I don't want to see him lose his family, lose this happiness that they deserve to have. If that was me, Brad …" She stopped talking, and he had to slide around to see her face. Her expression was filled with something so sad.

"You'd what, Emily, if that was you?"

Maybe it was the way he said it that had her eyes firing up again. "I love you, Brad Friessen, but a lie is a lie, and you can't have a marriage built on deceit," she said, and she slid back the covers and climbed out naked, striding into the bathroom and shutting the door.

EMILY HAD JUST FINISHED LOADING the dishwasher when Candy wandered in, holding Michael. He was cooing and giggling, and she was whispering something as she pretended to nip at his fists.

"Good morning, you two. How did you sleep?" Emily asked, seeing how happy Candy was. She'd never seen her this relaxed and comfortable with herself.

"Michael slept all night. It was wonderful." She glanced around. "Where is everyone?"

"Brad took the kids to school, and Neil tagged along and took Cat, too." She had to smother her laughter as she remembered the moment her husband realized he was going to have to take the minivan. Just watching him, her large, sexy husband, slip into that average, everyday gray van had been priceless. "Rodney and Becky took Brad's truck and are off visiting a neighbor down the road, so it's just us and that beautiful baby. There's coffee, and I can whip you up some eggs if you'd like."

Candy waved away the offer. "I'll grab some coffee."

Emily watched her, wondering if Brad would make the

effort to pull Neil aside and talk to him again. She hoped so.

"So how are you doing after last night?" Candy leaned against the counter, pouring her coffee.

Emily reached over and took the baby from her. "I'm good. There's cereal on the counter there. Help yourself."

She reached into the cupboard and grabbed a bowl, and Candy took it from there, filling it up and taking milk from the fridge. Emily pulled out a chair from the table and sat down, holding the baby in her arms. She found herself looking for Neil in this baby: the nose, the eyes, the smile. The expression around Michael's eyes was all Neil. How could Candy not see it? But then, had she really noticed herself before today?

"You were pretty upset last night. Neil explained to me about Crystal when he came to bed. I hope you don't mind?" Candy put the bowl of cereal and her coffee on the table and sat down, scooting her chair in closer.

"No, of course not. I just never expected her to show up here. Do you have any idea how hard it was to have a woman show up and say she's my kid's mother? I felt like a nobody. It hurt, after all she's done to come between me and Brad—all the work, and what I've done with Trevor … I'm his mother." When Emily glanced up, Candy had a shadow of hurt in her expression. How stupid could she have been? Of course Candy understood, after all she'd been through.

"Oh, I know, Emily. Believe me, I do," Candy said. Then she smiled so softly over at Michael. "It was something I worried about with Maria. She was horrible—horrible. I was so glad when she lost the baby. Does that make me a monster?"

Emily hoped her expression didn't show the alarm she felt racing through her.

"Emily, are you all right?" Candy asked just as the phone rang.

Emily jumped up and reached for the cordless phone on the counter, thankful for the interruption. "Hello?" she said as she faced Candy, who was taking a bite of her cereal while Emily held Michael.

"Emily, this is Roberta Steele at the school."

She turned away from Candy, staring at the wall, wondering why the school secretary was calling. "Is there something wrong?" She didn't know why she was feeling this panic, but then, every time Trevor's school called, it was always something—any manner of things that would have Emily driving to the school to pick him up.

"There's a woman here who says she's Trevor's mother."

She listened to the secretary, and she heard the words, but the alarm buzzing in her ears had the baby picking up on her distress. Maybe Candy noticed, as she suddenly took Michael from her.

"Let me guess. Blond hair, said her name is Crystal?" she snapped into the phone.

"Yes, that would be her, and she's standing right here. What would you like me to do?"

She couldn't believe the school was actually asking. "I am Trevor's mother. You tell her to leave. What is it she's trying to do? What does she want?"

The secretary cleared her throat. There was a rustling against the receiver, and she must have said something to Crystal, because when she came back on the phone, she said, "She wants to see him in his class, see how he's doing. I think, considering the confusion, I should have you and Mr. Friessen come in."

"Of course, we'll be there as soon as possible," Emily

said. When she hung up the phone, Candy was watching her closely.

"What's going on, Emily?"

"Crystal is at Trevor's school. I told Brad she was up to something, and he wouldn't believe me. I swear that woman is out to destroy our lives again."

Chapter 19

"Trevor seems so happy at school. You've really done something special for him," Neil said from the passenger side of the minivan. Cat was in a car seat in back. Brad glanced a couple times in the rearview mirror at the little girl, who seemed so happy and content.

"I could say the same about you and what you've done for Cat. That wasn't an easy road for her. I don't think I've ever heard you read so much before, and you're always talking to her and getting her to talk."

An easy smile touched Neil's lips. He was beginning to relax. His dark coat rustled as he rested his arm against the door. "Is there anything you wouldn't do for your kids?" Neil asked him.

Brad sent a quick glance over to his brother. "No, not where my kids are concerned," he said.

"Well, same here. I guess I never realized what Cat was going to need, but you're all of a sudden just living it and doing those necessary things that she needs for her brain to develop. She was denied for so long—I took so much for granted because I have all of my senses. I never understood how much more she needed, how important it is to always talk to her and read to her all the time, just to retrain her brain. There are things we take for granted, or always did, with kids who learn everything naturally: talking, walking, responding, reasoning … I saw you and Emily with Trevor, and it was so much work. That was all I saw until I was doing it with Cat. The first time I read a book to her and she smiled at me and responded to me, I knew then that I had been missing so much. ”

Brad didn't say anything as he watched his brother, who seemed to be working through something.

"I always thought Trevor was a burden for you."

He couldn't believe his brother had said that. He shot him another glance, squeezing the steering wheel a little harder.

"I was wrong. I'm sorry."

Brad didn't know what to say. Of all things, he never expected anyone in his family to say something like that, let alone believe it. "I don't know what to say, Neil. A burden, really?"

"Look, I was wrong. I was only seeing everything you had to do, the way he didn't understand things like other kids do. There was so much work involved in showing him how to do something when it would be easier to do it yourself."

"So what changed your mind?"

"Having Cat and finally understanding the other side. She works ten times, a hundred times, harder than any kid I've ever seen. She doesn't have it easy. The speech therapist makes her talk when she doesn't want to, when she'd rather just sign because she's tired. I never realized how far behind she was in everything else: dressing herself, eating, using a knife and fork … Just telling her things is a process that we have to walk through over and over, as her brain's learning to understand sound. I saw then what you and Emily do with Trevor, and it made sense. I didn't get it before."

"And you do now?"

"I do. I just never realized the advocate you have to be for Trevor, too, and how hard he has to work to learn something. You make him, and you follow through, and you've gotten him help. I've seen how far he's come. You and Emily have done a great job—"

Brad's cell phone rang, cutting Neil off. He reached into his coat pocket and glanced at the screen, seeing his home number. "Em, almost home," he said, pressing the phone to his ear.

"Crystal is at the school." She was close to freaking out. "The school called and said she's there."

"What?" It took him a second. Then he hit the brakes and pulled a U-turn on the road.

"Brad, what the hell is going on?" Neil said, his hand on the dash.

"I'm on my way back to school now. What the hell is she doing there, Em?" he shouted, but it wasn't her he was mad at, it was himself. He was furious with himself because his father, his brother, even Emily had warned him about letting Crystal back in.

"Come and get me!" She was angry, too. "I'm coming, and I'm stuck here because your mom and dad have the truck."

"No, you stay there. I've already turned around." The fact was that he didn't want her anywhere near Crystal. He needed to have a heart to heart with that woman, and the last thing he wanted was to see the hurt in Emily's eyes again.

There was silence on the other end.

"Em, I don't want you around her. I'll call you as soon as I'm finished with the school."

There was a click, and he realized she'd hung up on him. He held the phone out then dropped it into the cup holder.

"What's going on, Brad?" Neil said. "As if I need to ask. Crystal, right?"

"She's at the school. I don't know what she's doing there, but she's there. What next?"

Neil was shaking his head as Brad pressed the gas pedal, speeding up.

"Don't you dare say anything," Brad snapped. "Not a word."

Neil gestured vaguely at the road. "Not saying anything, Brad, but you fucked up when you opened that door."

Chapter 20

"Just remember—keep a cool head. Losing it isn't going to solve anything," Neil said from beside him, shoulder to shoulder, as he pounded the pavement at the front of the school. Cat was in Neil's arms, and thankfully the little girl had no idea what was going on.

He yanked open the main door and had only taken two steps to the office when he heard her voice. It was unmistakable, even after all these years. The softness, the directness, and the pitch in her voice would have once had him doing anything for her. Now, it filled him with dread.

As soon as Brad stepped inside the office, the secretary's eyes widened from where she was standing behind the desk. The principal, Allan Barber, a shorter man, balding, in his mid fifties, was also speaking with Crystal.

"What's going on here?" Brad said, and everyone turned to look at him. Crystal, her hair pulled back in a ponytail, was wearing a burgundy turtleneck, holding her black coat folded over her arm. She was wearing makeup, not heavy, but she wasn't the plain woman who had showed up yesterday. She looked at him, too.

"I came to see Trevor at school." Crystal faced Brad. She didn't smile, but she seemed determined about something.

"You came to see Trevor. I see. And why?" Brad said, brushing back his jacket and putting his hands on his hips as he took another step toward Crystal.

She looked up at him. She should have been terrified, but she held her ground. "He's my son, Brad, and I want to see him in school and see how he's doing, what he's learning."

For a minute, he had to fight the urge to laugh at her. Was she serious? He took in the expressions on the principal's and secretary's faces. They were uncomfortable.

"Mr. Friessen, your wife has been called, too," the secretary said, and Brad nodded curtly to the slender brunette.

"Mr. Friessen, maybe I could see you and Mrs. Friessen in my office?" the principal said. It took Brad a minute to realize he was referring to Crystal.

"Crystal is not my wife," he stated. He was glad, as he noted Neil's alarmed expression, that Emily wasn't here. He knew what that kind of comment, referring to Crystal as Mrs. Friessen, would do to Emily. She'd hold on to that hurt, which would begin to snowball if he didn't find a way to end this now and get Crystal out of their lives for good.

The principal started down the hall, and Crystal followed.

Neil touched his arm. "Brad, you need to call your lawyer," he said. He asked the secretary to stay with Cat, and there was a hesitation, but he didn't give the woman much choice. He signed something to Cat before putting her down on a chair.

Brad didn't say a word as he started down the hallway to the principal's office, Neil right behind him. When Neil closed the door, Allan glanced up, and, for a minute, Brad thought he'd ask his brother to leave. But there was no way he was going into anything with Crystal without someone watching his back.

"My brother stays," he said. "Crystal, I'm going to ask you one more time why you're here. You showed up yesterday and disrupted my household during Trevor's birthday party. You saw him, and I told you not to come back."

"I never agreed to that, Brad. I'm sorry, but after seeing Trevor yesterday and seeing how happy he is … he was talking. I know he wants to see me. He asked me to come back. I want to see him, too."

Was she serious? He could feel a twitch in his eye as he tried to reel in his instinct to shout, to yell.

"Crystal, you signed away your parental rights," Neil said from where he was leaning against the door. "Brad is the sole guardian, with sole custody. You can't come in here and disrupt Trevor's life, his wellbeing."

The principal went to sit behind his desk.

Crystal was standing off to the side, Brad facing her. "I'm still his mother," she said. "I have the right to school information regarding Trevor. I have the right to speak with his teachers."

"You have no rights. You signed away your rights." Brad actually took a step closer to her, and he felt his brother's hand on his arm.

"No, Brad, you're wrong. I may have signed over full custody and guardianship to you, but I'm still his mother, and I have the right to be provided with his medical and school information."

"She's right," the principal said. "There're federal laws in place that state equal access to education information has to be provided unless there's a court order revoking those rights." Allan gestured to Crystal and then to Brad. "Do you have a court order in place to this effect?"

What he had was a hole in his bank account after paying Crystal a pile of money to go away, to sign over full custody to Brad. She had no visitation rights at all, so he wondered for a moment if there was something he was missing. Had his lawyer missed something? "What is it you really want, Crystal? You've never given a damn about Trevor, and now suddenly, after all these years, you want what, exactly?"

His dad had been right. Neil's hand was on his arm again, and then there was a commotion in the hall and a knock on the door.

He turned as the door opened and Emily stepped inside, her hair hanging loose over her shoulders. She was wearing her brown sweater coat, and her blue eyes were far from those of the confident, loving woman he'd left this morning. Then he saw his dad behind her. For a minute, he considered asking Emily to wait outside, but he stopped himself the moment the words were about to leave his tongue. He held out his hand to her, and he could see the relief she tried to hide when she put her hand in his.

"Look, you two need to come to an understanding," Alan said. "I'm not getting into the middle of this." He flushed, taking in Emily. "Custody issues are difficult and messy at times. Trevor is in class right now, and I think it would be best if I leave you in my office to work out some mutual agreement regarding school."

Emily started to say something. He heard the gasp, her sharp intake of breath, and he squeezed her hand.

"School has been arranged by my wife, Emily. *She* is Trevor's mother. Crystal may have given birth to him, but—"

"Look, I don't want to do this," Alan said. "Work out

an agreement. Brad, you're the custodial parent. Emily, you've done so much for Trevor, and you're married to Trevor's father, which creates an even bigger gray area, but you don't have the right to make decisions for him. Federal law is clear that Trevor's mother here has the right to information. Brad, you are required to keep her informed, though I've yet to see a court enforce this. Come on, folks. I need you to sit down and work things out. Mrs. Fr—" He cleared his throat roughly. "Crystal, we can't have parents showing up whenever they feel like it to disrupt class, but I'm not about to ban you, either."

Emily's hand slipped from his, and she stood in front of Neil. Brad couldn't believe the nightmare Crystal had created here.

"Excuse me. I think maybe we all need to have a talk." It was Rodney who stepped into the overcrowded office, sounding tired and annoyed.

"I would really love that," the principal said.

Chapter 21

She wanted to weep, she wanted to hide. She had to fight the urge to race out the front door and leave this nightmare behind, all because it had just been pointed out, in an indirect way, that she had no voice in Trevor's care. She had been the one fighting with the schools, speaking for Trevor and making sure he got the help he needed. She had been the one who marked his progress, met with the teachers and his consultant, did all those extra things that had to be done so that Trevor could learn to do the things a typical child could, from tying his shoes and making his lunch to combing his hair and brushing his teeth. Here was Crystal, a woman who had done nothing other than give birth, and she had walked in here with more rights than Emily.

Oh, Allan hadn't come right out and said it, but he could barely look at her, with the awkwardness of this situation. Maybe it would always be this way, forever, a front line she would always tread. Was this what happened when families blended?

She took in the small, empty classroom that Allan had led them to. A big square table sat in the center, with wooden chairs stacked against the wall. It was a room she'd been in many times before when meeting with the school and teachers regarding Trevor.

Neil had left, taking Cat with him. It just wasn't doable, having her anywhere near this situation. Emily was grateful that Rodney had stayed.

Brad closed the door, leaving the four of them alone together. Crystal looped her coat over the back of a chair. The woman had an amazing figure. She was tall and slender—five foot six or seven, Emily figured—and she wore flats and dark blue jeans. She still looked so young.

Rodney gestured to Emily. "Come sit down." He actually pulled out a chair for her at the table and sat in the one beside her. Brad took the seat at the end of the table across from Crystal. Great, now they were all sitting.

"I need to say something," Crystal started, and Emily's stomach tightened as she looked right at her. "Emily, I would like to thank you for looking after Trevor and for all you've done for him."

What the hell was she saying? For a moment, Emily felt as if she was the hired help again.

Brad slid around in his chair and crossed his legs at the side, his arm resting on the table as he faced Emily. He seemed to tense before glancing across the table at Crystal. "What is it you really want, Crystal, money?" He shook his head. "We're divorced. Emily is my wife. She's Trevor's mother in every way that matters, and you come in here, disrespecting us, my family, my wife? No, I'm sorry, you're done. I want you out of here, and don't ever come back."

Crystal was sitting up ramrod straight. She was not a woman who could be pushed around. She had always been spoiled, strong minded, and conniving. She glared back at Brad with something in her expression that Emily had never seen before. "No, Brad. I have a home here now. I've put my life together, and I want to know my son. Whether you believe this or not, I made a lot of mistakes, and I regret my choices, but I can't go back and fix them. There isn't a moment that's passed that I haven't thought of Trevor, how he's doing. I want to be part of his life, to have some small piece of it. Maybe there's something I can do that would help him just a little bit." She put her hand on the tabletop and lowered her gaze as she gently rubbed a spot in the wood grain. Her mouth was open just a bit, enough that Emily could tell she was taking a minute before speaking again.

Emily glanced at her father-in-law beside her, who was sitting with his arms crossed, watching Crystal. Brad had a hint of pink in his cheeks and a fire blazing in his eyes. It was a wonder he hadn't tried to toss Crystal out. He was doing what he could to hold himself in check, but Emily was seeing her angry husband face off with the woman who had always pushed every one of his vulnerable buttons.

Emily had to clear her throat as she looked toward her husband. Of course, his gaze went right to her face, and his expression, all hard and unfeeling for Crystal, changed to something soft for her. She knew he loved her. She could see it in his expression. Then a bell sounded. Students were in the hallways, and there was noisy chatter and then a knock at the door.

"Hi, I heard you were here," came a voice from the doorway. Kim, Trevor's EA, walked into the room with Trevor behind her.

"Hi, Dad, Mom." He waved to Emily and Brad and

then saw his granddad, but the moment he saw Crystal, he walked over to her. "Mom, you came! Kim, this is my mom. She gave me the Lego mug." He was so happy, probably the only one in the room who didn't have a personal agenda.

Crystal slid back her chair, stood up, and went right to Trevor. She didn't hug him but touched his arm instead, and the way she smiled at him, as if she really did care, had Emily wanting to crawl away and weep. "I wanted to see your school, your class," she said.

"Okay," Trevor said. "Kim, can I show Mom my class?"

But Kim had finally figured out the problem. Maybe it was the horror Emily couldn't hide on her face that had Kim blushing, then saying, "I don't know if that's a good idea." She looked to Brad and then Emily for help.

But it was Trevor, who reached for Crystal's hand and started pulling her toward the door, who had Emily scraping back her chair and saying, "Yes, by all means, show Crystal your class, Trevor. I'm going home. I'll see you there."

Then Trevor went out the door, leading Crystal toward his class.

Emily gathered up her purse and said to Rodney, "Can you drive me home?"

"Em, I'm not leaving this school with Crystal here," Brad said. "I don't want her alone with Trevor." He was standing, and he was mad.

"Brad, you're right, you need to stay, but I can't and won't watch this anymore. It hurts too much. You need to fix this." She touched his hand.

"Em, I'm sorry. I didn't ask for this." He was furious.

"I know." She glanced over at Rodney, who was wiping

his face and then staring at the door as if working out a puzzle in his head.

"Brad, Emily's right. You need to stay. Whatever's going on with her, I think you're probably the only one who can find out."

As much as she didn't want to admit it, Emily knew Rodney was right.

Chapter 22

Brad was waiting for Crystal when she came out of Trevor's classroom just as the other kids started filing back in after recess. Maybe she hadn't realized that only Brad had stayed, as she immediately looked behind him.

"They're gone. It's just you and me, Crystal." He was leaning against the wall, looking down at her as she seemed to pull herself together, offering him a half smile as she gripped her coat.

"He showed me his journal and his artwork. I didn't realize he could draw, and his artwork, his colors … he's so good at what he does. He's doing well in school?"

He watched her swallow. Good, she was nervous, and she wasn't so good at hiding it. "He's doing as well as can be expected, Crystal. He has autism. He needs an aide who can help in the class, as he isn't independent, and he struggles here. He'd be lost in this classroom with all of the auditory instructions. Kim breaks things down, writes out instructions, whatever's needed so he can be successful."

She nodded, but he wondered whether she really

understood. He gestured for her to start walking, and thankfully she did. Down the hallway, glances were cast their way from passing teachers.

They went out the door of the school, where they stopped in the parking lot. She pulled a set of keys from her pocket and then slipped on her black coat. It was automatic when he reached out and helped her on with it. This was something his father had taught them first and foremost: They were gentlemen, and they always helped a lady with her coat.

"Thank you." She tossed him an easy smile.

"You're not going to leave, are you?" he said, knowing that whatever was going through her head, she'd decided nothing yet.

She just looked at him. "I was talking to some people, professionals, who said autistic children have behavioral problems and react differently to things, but Trevor seems so happy and calm. I remember when he was young, he would do the oddest things. He doesn't anymore?"

What was it about this woman he'd once loved, who'd turned his world upside down, that had him standing here, wanting to explain their son? "He has no behavioral problems. He adapts easily and doesn't freak out anymore, but make no mistake, Crystal: He works ten times harder than all of us just to do the same things we do easily, and just learning one simple task can sometimes seem insurmountable. He's very happy, and all of that is because of Emily. He's so lucky my wife is the person she is. She loves him, Crystal. She's his mother."

She nodded and looked away as if sorting something through her mind. "She doesn't seem your type. She's so … mousy."

What the hell was this? "Mousy? I guess I finally grew up and got past that superficial stage. Now I have something deeper. Make no mistake, though. My wife is anything but mousy."

Crystal gave him another odd look. "You look good, Brad." Then she looked away, and he wondered what her game was.

"What really brought you here, Crystal?"

"I was in an accident."

He watched her and wondered for a minute whether she was looking for sympathy.

"It wasn't bad or anything, but I broke my ankle and was laid up for a while."

"Sorry to hear that," he said, though he really didn't want to hear her sob story.

She glanced up at him again. "It seemed I was surrounded by people who were touched by autism. There was a woman with a teenager—I only saw him a few times, but he couldn't function alone. He carried this rubber ball around, and he had to have it or he'd start yelling and hitting his head with his hand. He couldn't talk much. His mother always had to hold his hand, and of course I thought of Trevor.

"Then I was shocked by this physiotherapist I met, a nice lady who told me she had autism. I began to notice things, like when there were too many people in a room and she would talk too loud, others would look at her as if she didn't understand social protocol—and she didn't. She was evaluated one day by the head of ortho. I remember she was so nervous, mumbling under her breath, and the way she walked with these tiny, fast steps behind him … it was so odd. She was hunched over, talking really fast about what she did, agreeing with him and repeating things he said, answering him almost in a way he would want to hear. It was all lies."

Brad couldn't help wondering why she would have

given someone like that the time of day. Crystal had always been about herself, what was in it for her, not helping others or giving a damn about anyone else.

Then she shrugged. "Then the doctor opened my chart and was pointing at something she'd written, questioning her about it. She started denying writing it. I had to get up and look, and I'm staring at her handwriting, and he's looking at her and knows she's lying, and she denies, and keeps denying. She even went so far as to say it was written by another resident who was jealous of her. I actually laughed, because she was serious.

"It was then that I started talking to this one psychologist who opened my eyes to autism. When you meet one person with autism, it's just one person. They're so different with how they react, respond, and mix with people. This woman, who was very good at her job of helping with my rehab, couldn't work with anyone else. She hated all the other medical staff, and no one liked her, either. They called her a psychopath and a pathological liar. They avoided her. This psychologist told me that many adults with autism in society today have trouble with relationships and can't relate to people on an emotional level, so they choose not to."

"So you have a friend with autism," he said.

"No, I couldn't deal with her, either. I hate her now, and I have to remind myself she has autism. She tried to take money from me, and even worse, she believed she was entitled to it. Her behavior wasn't sane. She made me nervous, because I realized then that everything she was saying was a lie, and to someone just meeting her, she was believable. Has Trevor … ?"

He knew what she was asking. This was the first time he'd seen her worry about someone other than herself. "No, Trevor doesn't lie, but he also doesn't understand how to relate to people. He learns routines, and he's good. He follows through, he's agreeable, he doesn't argue, he's compliant. Sometimes he'll say he didn't do something even though he did, but he understands that Emily and I won't tolerate that, so right after saying, 'I didn't do it,' he confesses. You have to know that Trevor has been in therapy since Emily got him started. It was what you tried to put a stop to."

She actually flushed. "I'm sorry. I'm not proud of what I did. I can see it's helped him."

"Yes, it has. He wouldn't be where he is today without his consultant and this program we run, with everyone working with him. The physiotherapist you met is probably a pretty good example of why early intervention is imperative. Trevor has to be able to get along with people to function in society. He has to learn how to fit in, to read people, to respond to their body language. It's foreign to many children with autism, and that's why everything has to be taught. If you don't, you end up with someone who'll never hold a job, who'll be miserable—and that's if they're high functioning, which Trevor isn't. Trevor will always have a family who'll be there to make sure he's okay and that he's never put in a situation he can't deal with."

She was watching him, her light blue eyes filled with sadness. She nodded. "I want to be a part of his life, Brad, and I would like you to consider where that could be."

He started to say no. Maybe she saw that, as she reached out and touched his arm. He heard a honk and glanced up to see his dad pull up to the curb, driving his truck.

"Please, Brad, don't write me off or brush me aside on this," she said. "Please, just take your time and consider it. There has to be some place in his life for me. He's my son, too, and whether you believe it or not, I do care, very much."

She didn't give him a chance to say anything, as she stepped off the curb, walked to her little dark compact, and climbed in.

Chapter 23

She loved her kitchen, her living room, and the miles of pasture that surrounded the house. She was living her dream, but darkness had tiptoed in from some place she didn't want to go, and it was messing with her happiness. She couldn't settle herself after Rodney dropped her at the door before turning around to go back into town and get Brad.

She should have felt bad, but she couldn't stay one more second at that school with Crystal. She was Trevor's mother, but for the first time she felt as if she was the other woman, without a voice. She had no legal rights with Trevor—that much had been made clear, albeit in an abstract way. It made no sense. She was the one in charge of his day-to-day care, of loving him, raising him, teaching him … and she had no authority.

She dumped her purse on the sofa table and heard footsteps on the stairs along with voices in Brad's office.

"You're back." Her mother-in-law, Becky, stepped off the bottom step, holding a baby monitor. She didn't say anything, but her expression held enough alarm that she had to be thinking the worst about their situation, which, as far as Emily was concerned, seemed about as bad as it could get.

"I am." She pulled off her sweater and stopped in front of the large gold-framed mirror, taking in her appearance. She had a round face and never wore makeup except when Brad took her out somewhere special, which wasn't often. Her brown hair was long and cut in layers so she could easily pull it back into a ponytail. She'd never liked the light smattering of freckles on her cheeks and nose, even though Brad thought they were cute, and she always wore such plain clothes, blue jeans and T-shirts. Even today, she didn't think she stood out. She was average, yet a man like Brad had fallen in love with her.

Becky put her hands on Emily's shoulders and was in the mirror behind her, peeking over her shoulder. "You're lovely," she said.

"Average, you mean."

She squeezed her shoulders. "No, you're by no means average. Any woman who can turn the head of my son and keep his interest the way you have … well, as a mother"—she was shaking her head at Emily, ready to scold her, she was sure—"you are truly the best. You're beautiful. Take a look in that mirror at how we see you. There's nothing plain or ordinary about you."

"But I'm not a beauty queen. I'm short, my nails are always a mess, and I don't wear heels or dazzling dresses. This is me—every day."

"Well, 'you every day' is a very special person, but I'm thinking maybe you want to add something to your relationship?"

Emily would have been embarrassed if it had been anyone else, but Becky seemed to understand how she was feeling. "I want Brad to be blown away when I walk in a room," she said, stopping herself from revealing that she wanted Brad's eyes to pop out of his head because she was so sexy. She wanted him to see her in some enticing little black dress, with pumps that showed off her slim legs, her hair in some updo that would have him drooling, and her makeup done tastefully. She wanted every man to stop and take a second look—but her husband would be the lucky dog. She wanted every man to know she was Brad's.

"I think what you and Brad need is time away alone together," Becky said, and Emily patted her hand.

"That would be nice, but we can't right now." She stepped away.

"Something will always come up, Emily. Life always launches curveballs your way, and it sometimes feels like the universe is messing with your happiness. You have to make the time and just do it. The problems will still be here, but sometimes you need to put them on hold and look after yourself and your man—reconnect. When you come back, those problems you left behind suddenly won't feel so insurmountable," Becky said, stopping suddenly to wince and press her hand to her lower back.

"Are you okay?" Emily reached out for her arm, but she just waved her away.

"Just my back's been giving me trouble, off and on. It'll be fine."

But Emily wondered. Watching Brad's mom this visit, she seemed to have aged. "Are you sure? Can I get you an ice pack or something?"

"No, it's fine. Just not used to carrying a baby around and playing with my grandkids."

She wasn't sure she believed her, but she wasn't about to push it. "Neil and Candy here?"

"Back in Brad's office. Go on, I'm going to make some

tea and take a moment for myself while Michael and Cat are napping."

Emily watched her stride into the kitchen. She might have lost some weight, not as plump as she remembered. The office had double glass doors opposite the separate dining room. Neil was sitting behind Brad's desk in the leather chair, his feet up on the desk, reclining, and Candy was sitting on one of the wingback chairs angled in front of the desk. They were chatting, and he started to lean forward when he saw Emily step inside.

"Emily, you're back. How are you?" he asked cautiously. She kept walking as Candy slid around.

"Hey, are you okay? Neil was just filling me in."

Emily sat in the other chair. For a minute, she just enjoyed being in a room together with Neil and Candy. "I had to leave," she said, not missing the exchange between the two. They were worried. "You two look so good together," she said then. "With everything going on, I just wanted you to know that I noticed, and I'm so happy that you two and your family are doing so well. Don't let anything come between you."

She could feel Neil's heavy gaze burning into her. Of course, he had to be wondering if she knew. She met the shrewdness that lingered there for a minute, and she hesitated.

Candy appeared confused, and Emily waved her hand. "I always thought that with where Brad and I were, we were untouchable, but I was wrong."

"Emily, Brad loves you. Don't let Crystal cast any doubts there," Neil said in a rather sharp tone.

"I know he does, but sitting at the school, I realized that as much as I believed I was Trevor's mother and in control of the situation, I'm the one person who has no control and no say at all, and it hurt." Still worse, though she didn't say it, was the knowledge that even though Crystal had signed away her rights, she still had more than Emily would if something ever happened to Brad.

"You're Trevor's mother, Emily, and I understand, maybe better than anyone, what you're going through," Candy said. "I can't imagine what I'd do if Cat's or even Michael's mother came back into the picture, but we've adopted Cat, and Michael is in the process." She stopped and looked to Neil, waiting for him to finish and fill in the blanks for her.

Neil was like Brad in many ways: smart, sharp, kind, and a good friend. But Emily could see a shrewdness there. He was a man with secrets, a man who did things his way, and she wondered whether some of that would eventually come back on him.

"It won't happen, Candy," Neil said. "Michael is your child, and you're his mother. Cat's, too. No one can come in and take them or tell you you have no say. Emily, Brad has got to finish this with Crystal. His lawyer needs to get this under control so that if something happens, you'd have guardianship of Trevor."

Maybe having Neil saying it out loud, this thing she'd feared for a while but had never allowed herself to think about, brought it all home. This was a place in her head where she didn't want to go. Candy gave Neil a disapproving look, and he gestured toward her.

"Look, she needs to know this," he said. "I'm sure my brother realizes now, this morning, that he needs to do something."

Emily could hear the diesel engine of the truck—Brad's truck. "Well, sounds like my husband's home. I guess I should find out what kind of chaos that woman wants to cause now."

Becky walked into the living room the same time Emily

did, just as Rodney and Brad stepped in the front door. It was one of those moments where she felt as if everyone was watching her. Maybe they were worried about her reaction, what she'd do or say, or maybe they were concerned about upsetting her further.

"So what does she want now?" she said. She stopped about a foot from Brad, far enough away that he couldn't touch her and close enough that she could read every part of his body language. She expected him to tense or to yell or at least be angry, but he took a breath and, in a voice that was so calm, said, "She wants to be a part of Trevor's life."

Chapter 24

No one said a word. Nothing. It was so quiet that, for a moment, Brad could hear the tick of the grandfather clock in the living room. Emily's eyes flared wide, and she gasped, then blinked as if trying to understand what he'd said.

"She wants to be a part of Trevor's life. In what way?" she asked calmly. That, of course, worried him.

He shrugged off his coat. Instead of hanging it in the closet, he walked over to Emily and tossed it over the sofa table, on top of her purse, then ran his hand over her arm just to touch her. It was the only thing he could think to do in that moment to reach her, to calm her. "She wants to be able to see him now and then, but she's left it up to me to decide how she can fit in." He could feel her start to pull away before she even took that first step, so he slid his hand under her chin so she had to look up at him. "This is our decision, Em, yours and mine."

She appeared surprised for a minute. "So if I tell you to get rid of her, make her go away and make sure she can never see Trevor again, you will?"

"You're my wife, and I'll do anything for you and the kids. You know that, right?"

She rested her hand on his wrist, but not to step away from him. He actually felt her giving in a little.

"So, yes, Em, you tell me what you want, and I'll make it happen."

She shut her eyes, maybe from relief. When she looked up at him again, the wall she'd slowly erected, built from all those painful memories, had crumbled. "What do you want to do, Brad? What possible benefit is there to her having any part of Trevor's life?"

"It's another relationship for him, though I don't know if she has what it takes to stick with it. Can it hurt for her to see him?"

"I don't want her back in our life, Brad. I can't believe someone like her can change. She's hurtful and conniving. I don't trust her," she said.

Emily was a smart, beautiful woman, and he admired her so much.

"I don't, either, but it may be too late for that, too," he said. "Trevor knows about her now."

Emily was shaking her head, and Brad could feel everyone watching them. Neil was standing with Candy in his arms, watching them, as were his mom and dad.

"Look, I know you all think I created a big mess here by opening this can of worms, and maybe I did. I can't take it back."

"No, you can't, and by the looks of it, Crystal has no intention of just walking away," Rodney said. "You saw her, Brad, her determination when she showed up at the school. Why?" He was shaking his head. "Your son wants to see her now, but how long do you think that will last?"

"Caring for an autistic child isn't easy," Emily said. "Trevor isn't easy, he's a lot of work. Why she insists she needs to be here, I don't know, but, Brad, I need to have some assurances for myself. If something happened to you, I … God help me, I hope nothing ever does, but what about Trevor then? I'm not his legal guardian, and I need to have something there. Having her come back now has made it perfectly clear that I have no rights, not with Trevor. You do, she does, I don't."

He'd never once considered the legal side for Emily. He was the head of the household, and he had full custody and guardianship. "You're right, Em, but the same holds true for Katy. She sees her dad—what, every month or so? Less and less. I think of her as mine, you know that. I need that authority there, too."

"Maybe what you two need to do is get your lawyer to take care of matters so the kids are protected," Neil said. "Establish guardianship with the courts if you need to. Take care of it now so you don't have to worry down the road."

Brad wondered for a moment if Neil was giving all this advice to try to help them fix a problem he couldn't fix in his own life. He slid his arm around Emily, and she easily went against his side. "The thing is that Crystal may have an interest now, but she'll get bored soon and leave."

"I don't want Trevor hurt, Brad," Emily said.

"I know you don't, and we're going to try to make sure he's not. We're going to set some ground rules. She follows them, or she doesn't see him." He could see how much Emily didn't want this to happen.

"We don't have a choice, do we?"

He rocked with her in his arms. "We have a lot of choices. I can tell her no, but Trevor will ask, and she may try to show up again. I don't want her confusing Trevor. It's up to you before, and if, we allow her one moment with Trevor."

Neil and his dad were watching him, their expressions grim. "You let her back in, Brad, and you're asking for trouble," Rodney said. "A person like that doesn't change overnight. You better make sure she can't pull the rug out from under you again."

Brad knew what his dad was saying. Crystal was smart —but he was smarter.

Chapter 25

"Is my mom coming, Mom?" Trevor was pacing back and forth in the living room. He'd put on his good jeans and his favorite blue and white striped polo shirt. He'd combed his hair with a part on the side, and he paced with his hands behind his back.

Brad was in the doorway, leaning, waiting. Neil and Candy had taken Katy, little Becky, Cat, and Michael out to the park in town and to run some other errands. Emily knew this was meant to reduce the tension in the house. Rodney and Becky had a flight back to Cancun this morning, and though they'd offered to stay, Brad had told them it was probably better if they didn't. He had a lot to take care of, including getting his lawyer working on legal guardianship agreements for both Trevor and Katy. Keith was working on it now, and as far as Emily knew—and Brad had assured her—Keith expected no issues, considering both Emily and Brad had sole custody of their kids.

It had seemed as if things were getting settled, but then Emily had watched as Rodney and Neil closed themselves up in Brad's office for an hour. What they talked about, she didn't know, and even Candy had been puzzled, only saying that Neil and his dad still had some things to work through.

Emily had already straightened the living room up, dusted the end tables, and plumped the pillows. She, too, was now wearing a path on the floor. She exchanged a few glances with Brad. He'd said twice that it would be all right, but having a woman she truly hated coming into her home and being with the boy she'd raised was a hard pill to swallow.

"She's here," Brad said in a low voice to Emily, but Trevor was excited and raced to the door.

"She's here!" he shouted as he pushed open the screen door and walked out.

"Trevor, shoes," Emily called out

"Oops, sorry." He came back in the house, and Brad rested his hand on his son's shoulder. "What are you planning with Crystal, Trevor? Do you want her to come inside, or did you want to show her around?"

"I want to show her the new calf."

"Then go get your boots and your coat." Brad rustled his hair.

"Dad, you messed up my hair," Trevor said as he walked to the back door, flicking his fingers through his hair to straighten it.

Emily could hear the footsteps on the porch and went to Brad's side, slipping her hand into his as he pushed open the screen door.

Crystal had on a cream sweater, a black broom skirt, and flat black suede boots with fringes. "Hi," she said with a smile. She looked nervous. She may have been trying to hide it, but she wasn't having much luck. She wiped her feet on the mat and stepped inside. "Is he here?"

Brad gestured to the kitchen. "He's getting his coat and boots on. He said he wants to show you the new calf."

He wasn't sure what he expected. Crystal hated everything about ranching: the animals, the smell, and the peaceful, quiet countryside. She had always been about nightlife and parties and people, and he wondered how she'd handle a rowdy baby calf.

"I'll leave my purse here, if that's all right?" she said.

Brad looked to Emily, but she couldn't say anything for a minute. "That's fine, Crystal," he replied, and he squeezed his wife's hand.

Then Trevor clomped into the living room, his boots thudding with each step. "Mom, you're here." He was so excited, and Crystal grinned at him in a way that made Emily wonder what was going through her head. She was genuinely happy to see Trevor, and she tucked her long blond hair, which was hanging loose, behind her ears. She had big gold hoop earrings and high cheekbones, but her makeup was lightly done. She was a beautiful woman. Emily had always envied that.

"Hey, look at you. I'm so happy to see you, and I'm so glad your dad …" She hesitated and then glanced over at Emily. "And Emily here said it was all right for me to see you."

"Thanks, Mom." Trevor patted Emily's back.

The light in his eyes for her made her want to kick herself for her jealousy. That kind of love didn't disappear. She was his mom, and he knew it.

"Do you want to see the baby calf?" he asked Crystal, but he didn't wait for her answer, as he was already out the door. "Mom, Dad, are you coming, too?"

Emily looked to Brad, who said, "Yeah, we are, bud. You take Crystal into the barn, but don't open the stall door, you understand?"

"Okay, Dad." He waved and started down the steps, and Crystal wore a puzzled expression.

"I didn't give him my answer," she said as she pushed open the screen door to follow him.

"No, he wasn't interested in waiting. It wasn't really a question for him, Crystal," Emily said, and she gestured after him. "You'd better hurry. He's halfway to the barn."

The screen door slapped closed behind Crystal, and she hurried to catch up with Trevor then walked side by side with him, his arms swinging, looking at each step.

Emily could see his mouth moving. "Oh, geez, he's counting his steps." She felt herself being pulled back to Brad, and she felt his hand over her stomach before he nuzzled her ear.

"Get your shoes on and your coat. It'll be fine. This is a good thing, for her to see everything today. We need to just hang back and watch," he said.

When she glanced up at Brad, she was no longer worried because Crystal was here. She only took a second to slip on her shoes, and Brad held her sweater up so she could slip it on. He took her hand again as they went out the back door, and they took their time walking to the barn, side by side.

"And this is BJ. He's new," Trevor announced from the barn. Emily could hear the excitement in his voice. Happy Trevor was loud and confident.

"How old is he?"

She could see them inside the barn, looking over the stall door.

"Good," Trevor said, and Crystal looked at him again and said, "I asked you how old he is. When was he born?"

Crystal was leaning against the stall, looking at Trevor, who took a step back and then fisted his hand to his mouth to clear his throat as if getting ready to announce something. Then he pointed at the ground. Crystal looked down and then over at Brad and Emily. Of course she was confused, so they walked in closer.

"Trevor, Crystal was asking how old the baby calf is," Emily said. "When he was born—which means, is he one week old, two weeks old? On which day last week was he born?" She was trying to prompt him, as he needed that sometimes.

"A long time ago," he said.

"It wasn't that long ago," she replied. "Which night did your dad wake you up so you and Katy and Becky could see the calf being born?"

Trevor was thinking. "Sunday," he said.

"That's right," Emily said. "Crystal, Trevor doesn't understand time. We're still working on it. He's mastered the days of the week, but this is one thing he's having trouble grasping. The months and weeks are too abstract for him."

She nodded. "Oh, okay."

Then Trevor started walking away, and Crystal's eyes went wide. She gestured helplessly as if to say, "What happened?"

"Hey, Trevor, you left Crystal over at the stall," Brad said. "She came to see you, bud."

"Oh, sorry." He turned around. "Do you want to see my new Star Wars Encyclopedia?"

"Sure I would," she replied, and when she followed him to the house, he started asking her about movies and video games, and she kept saying that she was sorry, but she'd never heard of any of them.

Chapter 26

The screen door squeaked as it slid open. Brad turned around to see Crystal step out. He could hear clattering from inside the house and knew Emily had started dinner.

"You're done?" he asked as she stepped out, clutching her purse, her lips tight.

She stopped in front of Brad and seemed to be struggling with something. "I am. It was good to see him. He looks so good. He's happy, I can see that."

Brad just watched her, wondering what was going to come next.

"I guess I never appreciated what you've done for Trevor," she said.

"That's all Emily, Crystal. My wife is a saint. Trevor wouldn't be anywhere without her," he said. He could see her discomfort in her slight flush.

"It's hard for me to see you so happy. Trevor's so happy, and you have this family who loves you. I guess I just wanted someone for me. Trevor loves Emily. He mentioned her and you and his sisters—in between video games and movies. Oh, and then he imitated some bird sound. I'm not sure what that was. He would show me things and tell me Emily gave them to him, or that she'd made them for him, and he calls her Mom …" She stopped talking and stared out into the front yard.

"She is his mom, Crystal. He knows it, and you should know that my lawyer will be calling you so that there will never be a question as to whether Emily's his mother. She'll be his guardian, too. Please don't fight it," he said.

He wasn't sure what he expected, but she seemed to have expected this, and she nodded.

"You're not coming back, are you?" he asked. He realized that maybe they'd come to an understanding, as she rubbed her mouth and chin with her fist and then slowly shook her head.

"I can't give him what he needs. I don't know how many questions I asked him, but he didn't answer me. He just walked away. Did he not hear me, or maybe he didn't understand … ? I don't know. I felt lost and just wanted to be able to connect with him, and I couldn't figure it out. He's connected to Emily, to you, to your family. I heard him, just now, go in and ask Emily what was for dinner and if he could help her. He left me as if he didn't realize I was still here …"

"Hey, Trevor has come a long way, but make no mistake: He has a long way to go. We have authority in his life. We hold him accountable, and he knows what we expect of him and that he has to answer to us. Someone new with him has to prove themselves to him. We've been working his program for years, and this has become second nature for us. It's part of our family, of who we are. We know how to redirect Trevor. Maybe now isn't the time for you to have a relationship with him. Don't make yourself feel guilty about it."

She was nodding. Her eyes were red, as if she was fighting to hold back tears. "I need to say goodbye to him. Would you keep me updated on how he's doing, his progress?" she asked, and he could see her holding it together. Whatever had happened to this woman, to bring her to the point where she appeared to care for someone other than herself, had his heart softening.

"Yeah, we'll let you know—but, Crystal, you can't show up whenever you want. Leave him be. He won't ask for you or worry about you. You need to know that. You can't disrupt his life."

She frowned and then shook her head. "I understand."

Brad started into the house, holding the door open for Crystal.

She shook her head. "Could you send him out?"

He watched her, taking in an uncertainty he'd never seen in her before. He then realized that she carried sadness, loneliness. "Yeah," he replied.

Chapter 27

She was stunned, speechless, when Brad appeared in the kitchen.

"Trevor, Crystal is leaving," he said. "She'd like to say goodbye to you."

Trevor was setting the table, and he put down the plates. "Okay." He didn't hesitate as he started toward the door, his strides confident, his arms swinging with purpose.

The expression on Brad's face had her turning away from chopping vegetables. "What's going on?" she asked.

"She's leaving, and I guess she realized Trevor needs more help than she can give. You were right about not stepping in and letting her see Trevor without help, letting her figure out that it's not that easy."

"So does this mean she's gone for good, or is she going to keep showing up?"

Brad shook his head and reached for Emily's hand, taking her with him to the window in the living room. "She's not ready to have the kind of relationship he needs to have. She wants to know how he's doing, for us to send updates and keep her in the loop."

"Will she interfere?" She had to know, but she wondered, as she watched Crystal outside with Trevor. She was looking at him, facing him, and Trevor was looking at the ground. Emily knew he wasn't really listening to what she was saying.

"No, she's lost right now. She doesn't understand what to do with him, how to be with him or talk to him. I think she thought it would be easier, but she doesn't really know him or what he needs. She just had to see it for herself. How did you know?" Brad asked her.

"Because it always looks easier on the outside looking in, but she's not here every day, working with Trevor. She doesn't know that certain questions are too abstract for him. She doesn't understand that when he walks away without answering, she has to follow through. She hasn't walked our walk with Trevor, talking him through a task when he doesn't understand, rewording what we say so he gets it. She wouldn't know where to start with him. Not many people do. They see how good he is with us only because he understands our expectations of him. We have authority in his life. She hasn't earned that, she's a novelty to him, she's interesting," Emily said. She loved the feel of Brad's large hand, twining her fingers with his, feeling the roughness of his skin—her husband, whom she loved deeply.

"You're a smart woman, Mrs. Friessen." He pushed open the screen door, leading her out behind him.

Crystal glanced their way for a second as she stood on the ground at the foot of the steps. Trevor had his back to them. She put her hands on his shoulders and rubbed.

"I love you," she said to him, and then she leaned in and hugged him, resting her head against his chest.

Trevor reached around and patted her back. "It's okay, Mom."

When she pulled away, looking at him and then up to Brad and Emily, Emily could see a mother's sorrow in her eyes. Trevor would never be hers, and maybe that was what Emily could see in the glossy sheen of her tears. Crystal had finally understood she couldn't just walk back in. The bond Trevor had with them was unbreakable.

"Will you call me, email me, and tell me how you are?" she said to Trevor.

She could feel Brad tense beside her, and she squeezed his hand to stop him from saying anything, because it was then that Trevor patted Crystal's arm and gestured to Emily.

"Mom will do it," he said. "Mom, call Crystal, okay?" Then he started back up the steps and stopped beside Emily. "Is dinner ready?"

She could hear a vehicle, and she looked up to see her minivan, driven by Neil. "Almost," she said. "Finish setting the table and wash up."

"Okay." Trevor went into the house, and Crystal was still standing there, looking lost.

"I'll send you my contact information," she said, looking first to Brad and then to Emily before taking her keys from her pocket and walking away.

Neil said something to her as she walked past him to her car. The girls climbed out of the minivan, and Candy lifted the baby out. Then Crystal was backing out and driving down the driveway.

"Dinner ready?" Katy asked, holding Cat's hand. Becky raced up the stairs with her.

"As soon as you all wash up," Emily said. "Go."

The chatter was lively as the girls stomped into the house.

"Everything went well?" Candy asked from where she

lingered beside her, Neil watching them from the foot of the stairs.

"My wife is brilliant," Brad said. He let go of her hand and slipped his arm around her shoulder, pulling her closer. She fit right beside him so easily as she slid her arm around his waist. "Crystal realized Trevor needs more than she can give him. She was lost and didn't know what to do when Trevor didn't answer her and started going off topic, fixating on video games and movies. My wife said to just stand back, don't do anything, and she knew exactly how Trevor would respond and what he would do. I guess I should have seen it."

Neil had the most engaging, handsome smile of all the brothers, and he turned all of it on Emily. He didn't say a word as he looked up at Candy then. "Should we tell them?" he asked.

Candy was holding a sleeping Michael. "Yes."

"What gives?" Brad asked.

"We're looking at a place not far from here. Took the girls with us to see it today. Remember the Graham place?" Neil said.

"That's on the other side of town, old house, how many acres?"

"Fifteen. House was renovated last year, small, four bedroom. It's by the ocean," Neil added, and Candy sent him a teasing smile.

"It's lovely. It's a home, Neil. We don't need anything bigger. Besides, we've been living in an apartment for … how long? Although it's nice, I'd like to have my horse and donkey back. Besides, my husband is refusing to go back to Cancun."

Emily looked up at Brad, although he didn't give anything away, and they both had a pretty good idea of why Neil didn't want to go back.

Michael started fussing and let out a wail. "He's hungry," Candy said, sliding her hand into his sleeper, "and wet. I'm going in to change him and heat up a bottle."

Emily didn't move. She listened to the voices of her children and watched Candy as she climbed the stairs and disappeared inside.

Neil glanced away awkwardly. "Did you tell Emily?"

"She's my wife, Neil. I don't keep secrets. It won't go anywhere."

Neil nodded.

What Brad hadn't said was that she hadn't given him a choice. She had nagged and prodded until he finally gave in and told her.

"You're hiding, Neil. That's what this is really about, isn't it?" Brad said, and Emily wondered how far Neil would go to protect his family.

"Maybe. But right now, Brad, I have my wife back. We have two kids we're going to raise here, and we're a long, long way from anyone who could try to disrupt my family's happiness. I'll move us across the world if I have to, just to make sure no one ever tries to come between me and my family again."

Maybe no one would ever be able to convince Neil to come clean with his wife, but Emily also understood that not everything was black and white. It was wrong to lie, but everything he'd done was because of his love for Candy. She prayed it wouldn't blow up in his face. "So are you putting in an offer on the house?" she asked.

He squinted into the setting sun. "Already did."

"Well, I have to say it'll be really nice to have you and Candy here." Emily nudged Brad, and he grunted.

"Yeah, I guess I can handle having your ugly mug

around here for a while yet. I take it you're not going back to Arizona?"

"Just to pack up, and I promised Candy I'd bring her horse and that damn nuisance of a donkey up to her. She loves them, and she misses them. Can I leave Candy and the kids here when I go?" He started up the steps.

Brad slipped his other arm around his brother as they started toward the door. "Hey, you don't need to ask that. She's family." Brad glanced for a second at Emily, and she realized he was giving her a say. He must have known how she felt.

"Neil, go take care of what you need to. Your family will be looked after here, always."

"Thanks, Emily."

Then the door burst open as Katy and Trevor poked their heads out. "We're starving! Aren't we having dinner?"

"Yes, dinner is ready. Let's go," Emily teased her kids as she followed them into the house and then turned to face the door, taking in the moment Brad said something to Neil and hugged him. Whatever passed between them, Emily knew the most important thing was always love.

Chapter 28

"Good God, woman. What are you wearing?"

Emily didn't just feel good, she felt sexy, desired, and wanted in a way she'd never experienced before in her entire life. She stepped into the living area of the suite that overlooked the blueness of the sea, moving carefully in the four-inch heels she'd had to practice walking in. It was breathtaking, the view of this island of Santorini. This trip had been a gift from Becky, fifteen days on a beautiful, romantic island about 120 miles southeast of mainland Greece. It was private, away from the beaches and tourist areas, with a view that had to be on everyone's bucket list. Having Neil and Candy staying at the ranch, watching the kids, and running things for Brad and her had allowed them to freely enjoy this time without worrying.

She took another careful step in the silver strappy shoes. She'd never worn anything like this before, and she'd squeezed herself into that little black dress, an asymmetrical design on the shoulder straps and cut just so, indecently showing enough breast and cleavage that her husband should be panting. She looked good, hot, sexy, and had taken time with her makeup and her hair, pinning it in a sexy updo.

"You like?" she asked, taking another step on the sexy heels. Brad's eyes took in all of her possessively, indecently, from the tips of her toes, to her breasts, to her lips, to her eyes as she stepped closer still.

He was in a white shirt, the top two buttons undone, his dark chest hair teasing her from the open V. He was barefoot in dark dress pants, and when his eyes lingered on hers, she knew Brad was seeing her in a way he never had before. "Hell, yeah. What are you wearing under that?"

She stepped closer still and rested her hands on his chest, offering him a flirty smile, stripping away whatever vulnerability may have lingered in her mind about her lack of sexiness, because this time with Brad was magical. It was the honeymoon they'd never had, and she planned to experience all the pleasures of her husband in ways they couldn't at home, not with three children running around.

She hadn't hesitated to order the sexy black lace underwear and matching bra that displayed her breasts to her husband in a way he wouldn't be able to resist. She loved pulling on the black sheer thigh-high stockings, assured by the lady at the lingerie store that men went crazy over them. For Emily, these fifteen days away with her husband would be about taking their passion, and their relationship, to a level they'd never been at before.

"There's only one way to find out," she whispered, staring at his lips before taking in the heat and passion flaring down at her.

"Hmm, should we eat first or later?" he asked, but she wasn't sure it was a question, as he leaned in and sampled what she offered. He pulled away, breathless. "Later it is. I love you, Mrs. Friessen."

She pressed closer to her husband, her breasts into his chest, feeling how much he wanted her. "I know," she said before he kissed her deeply again.

Turn the page for a sneak peek of
A DIFFERENT KIND OF LOVE the next book in *THE
FRIESSENS: A NEW BEGINNING*
Available in print, eBook and audio

A Vow of Love

A FRIESSEN FAMILY CHRISTMAS

—*"Absolutely brilliant. Got my coffee, said to hell with the house-work, and devoured it slowly. I was gobsmacked at Rodney's story. Poor Becky. This family series is a bloody good read. Thank you."*

—*"Compelling, emotions run high throughout this story."*

BOOKZILLA

—*"Neil and Candy have had a dynamic relationship with a lot of passion and disappointments. Can true love and a renewed trust get them their happy ever after?"*

J. MURPHY

—*"Loved this so much! Neil and Candy have such a special love that has touched me and even more so now. This book is a must read!"*

SUSAN

—*"I read this book in less than 24 hours on my vacation with my husband and two year old. I couldn't put it down, I have already fallen in love with Becky and had to see what happened with Maria. Loved it." – Amanda*

—*"The Friessen family is a family that really touches my heart and they will touch yours heart too."*

Sometimes families need a helping hand

Holidays are about family, love, and giving, but this Christmas, the Friessens are in for a rough holiday season.

Thirteen days before Christmas, a letter arrives that Candy Friessen was never meant to see. When she opens it, she discovers a lie that rocks her world, and she begins to question everything she and Neil have created together, including his love for her and their family.

Seven days before Christmas, her heart breaking, Candy considers leaving her husband for good, and she begins making plans—until a call one night alerts all the Friessens that Becky, their mother, is in the hospital, fighting for her life. Without a second thought, the entire Friessen clan is on a plane to her bedside. Faced with uncertainty, Brad, Neil, Jed, and their wives are together for Christmas, but there's no happy celebration, no gifts piled under the tree.

For Candy and Neil, once trust is destroyed, can their family bond be strong enough to save their marriage?

Chapter 1

Would she ever get used to this cold, damp weather? Candy pulled at the collar of her thick wool sweater and rubbed her arms as a chill went through her. She pulled back the curtains and took in the steady drizzle of rain over the brown fields, which she supposed would be green come spring. These were fields Neil had promised to fence in, where her horse and donkey could one day graze. As she took in the heavy blanket of clouds that filled the sky, turning it a dreary gray, she wondered how long it would take her horse and donkey to acclimatize. After the hot days of Cancun, Mexico, life in the Pacific Northwest would be a rude shock, she was sure. Would they miss the sun as she did? It had been so long since she'd seen it. After endless days of rain, she missed the brightness of it against the crystal blue ocean, the warmth, and her animals. Even though this property was oceanfront, it was darker, different—colder.

Neil had been on the phone, making arrangements to close up their Arizona apartment and to have everything shipped to their new home, an acreage outside Hoquiam,

Washington, in the Pacific Northwest. It was close to Brad and Emily and to the family home where Neil had grown up. This was a new beginning for them and their children, and she never questioned his need for a fresh start. She could leave everything behind, except for her horse, Sable, and her donkey, Ambrose, whom she'd rescued as a newborn after his mother was killed on the side of the road. She still couldn't believe all the hoops Neil had to jump through to move her animals up here. Passports for animals? She'd never heard of such a thing, and Neil was just ending his call with a customs broker, compiling all the paperwork that was involved.

"Candy, didn't you hear me call you?" Neil was standing in the middle of their sparse living room. It was finished in light woods and currently held a lone black easy chair, which was the only furniture they had. It had been brought over by Neil's brother Brad to tide them over until their furniture arrived. They could have stayed with Brad and Emily, but Neil insisted after purchasing this house that they all needed space, they needed their own home. Not for the first time, Candy disagreed, but she said nothing. There was something about Neil: Once he set his mind to something, no one could change it. She sensed this was more about his needs, as there was a tension she couldn't put her finger on between him and his brother.

"Sorry," she replied. She swallowed as she watched Neil, his dark hair a little on the longish side, touching the top of his ears with a natural wave she hadn't seen when he kept his hair short. Threads of gray were now woven through his thick hair—even more this morning, as if it had happened overnight.

"The kids asleep?" He glanced at the carpeted stairs and the open railing leading to the second floor.

"Cat's sleeping in our bed," Candy said, referring to an

air mattress on the floor. Their new bed, along with a kitchen table, a living room suite, and a bed for Cat, would be here Friday. Just two more nights of rambling through an empty house. "Michael's only been quiet a few moments," she continued. "I hope he's sleeping. He's been so fussy lately. He didn't sleep much last night." At least he was sleeping in his own bed, a crib, the one given to them by Brad and Emily.

Neil didn't say anything about the baby. If it had been Cat having trouble, he probably would've gone to check on her. The difference wasn't lost on Candy. He seemed so distracted as he glanced down at the paper he was holding. "The broker needs papers on Sable—registration, birth date. Since there aren't any, I need to at least know where you purchased him so that I can trace the paperwork. Ambrose, since you had him from birth and found him abandoned, is a little trickier ..."

She had her back to Neil and parted the sheers again, looking out at the steady rain. The day was so gray and depressing. Maybe it was the lingering silence that made her realize Neil was no longer talking. When she faced him, he was watching her in that way he had when he was trying to get into her head.

"What's wrong?" he said. He knew her too well, and sometimes she supposed that wasn't a good thing. There were times she needed space, but Neil wasn't a man who would give it to her.

"Tired is all, and cold." She shivered again.

Neil, too, was wearing a thick dark blue sweater and faded jeans. "We're just not acclimatized yet. You'll get used to it." He glanced at the fireplace. "A fire will help cut through the dampness. I'll call Brad later, get some wood from him." He went over to the wall, plain white, and touched the thermostat. "I can turn up the heat, but it's already as high as it should be."

"No, it's fine. It'll get too warm upstairs. Neil, even if there was paperwork for Sable, everything would have been lost in the storm. He was a gift from my dad. I don't know where he purchased him. Is that a problem?" She hoped it wasn't. Worry nagged at her. Would she ever see her horse and donkey again?

Neil started toward her and touched her arm, sliding his large hand over her shoulder and caressing her. He was so close, and she loved when he touched her like this. He didn't need to say anything to let her know how he felt about her. Their love was strong, and this bond between them … she knew deep in her soul that it was unbreakable. They'd been tested by things other couples hadn't, and she believed that had made them stronger, more connected. Nothing could ever come between them. "Neil, am I going to get Sable and Ambrose back?"

"Of course." The way he said it, she believed him. But then, Neil had this way about him. When he put his mind to something, he could move mountains. At the same time, she believed he'd do anything for her now. "I'll just have to be creative, is all. Don't worry about it. I'll find a way."

"Are you still planning on leaving Monday? What if you can't get the paperwork together, what then?"

Neil rubbed her arm, touching her still. He was right in her space, taking over as he always did, trying to fix everything for her. He ran his hand under her chin, and she had to look up. He was so tall. So was she, but he was amazing. Strength oozed from him. "I'll have it together," he said. "Don't worry. The guy I hired is good. Don't lose faith in me."

She had to hide her smile. Did he have no idea of how she believed in him? He was her hero, a man she looked up to, with all his flaws and bossiness. She truly believed that after finding their way back together, they wouldn't allow anything to come between them again. Neil had done that once, and it had almost destroyed her, but she could see his regret and feel his determination. It was unsettling but comforting to know she was loved so much.

"Are we ever going back to Cancun?" she asked. It wasn't that she wanted to go back. Cancun was filled with memories of hurt and betrayal—memories of the surrogate who had almost destroyed what Neil and Candy had.

Neil's expression darkened. "No, it's time for a new life here. We're done in Mexico."

She nodded. Maybe that was what she needed to hear, just a confirmation. At times, though, she couldn't shake the sense that they were hiding from something. "What about the resort, Neil? You haven't talked about it lately. Don't you need to be there to run the day-to-day operations? I know this was a really big deal for you."

The resort was being built on the oceanfront property that had once been hers. After a storm destroyed her home and she lost the land to her creditors, Neil had bought it and given it back to her. She had believed she couldn't live without it, but she was wrong. Her family was more important, and her life with Neil.

"I wanted to talk to you about that," he said. "It may be time to sell."

Was he serious? She had never seen him look so disinterested. After all the years of wanting that property, obsessing about building his resort—a resort that had been the biggest obstacle between them— he wanted to walk away now?

"I don't understand, Neil," she said. "Why would you sell it? You promised me a part of the beachfront would always be mine. You know how much it means to me."

"I won't sell if you don't want me to, Candy, but I don't see a reason to keep it. Our life is here now. Think about it. I don't plan on going back. We need to cut ties, sell, and move on with our lives."

She could hear Michael whimpering from upstairs. She sighed, and maybe it came out sounding uneasy, but she hadn't meant it to. She loved her baby, their baby, the little boy they'd adopted, but she was so tired. Michael had been more and more demanding as of late. "I'd better get him," she said.

She knew he wouldn't wake Cat, their deaf little girl, whom she'd found in a Mexican orphanage. Cat was such an inspiration to Candy, and she loved watching Neil with her, fussing over her, talking to her, reading to her when her cochlear implant was on. He did everything he could for a little girl he had wanted nothing to do with in the beginning. On the other hand, she'd yet to see him fuss over Michael, their baby, which was disconcerting. Maybe from the way Neil appeared distracted, not glancing at the stairs, she knew he wouldn't go up—not for Michael. For Cat, he'd already be taking the stairs two at a time. She should talk to him about it and make him listen this time, make him tell her why he was so distant when he'd been the one so obsessed with the idea of having a baby.

He waved the paper in the air. "I need to make some more calls," he said, then he left the empty living room through the kitchen, the floor creaking under his heavy footsteps to the small office at the back of the house, which still held a desk left by the prior owners. It was made of solid wood, old, probably something even Goodwill wouldn't want.

"Coming, baby," Candy called out as if that would reassure Michael, and she started up the stairs just as he let out a wail.

All Trinity Cooper Wilde wanted was a quiet Christmas alone with her baby, a baby no one knows about but her twin sister, Dawn.

Dawn has warned Trinity that she needs to come clean and tell everyone about the baby, including the father, Garrett Franke, their former neighbor, whom Trinity has hated since tenth grade—with the exception of one night last year, a mistake.

Her family is starting to wonder why she hasn't come home to visit in over six months, and Trinity knows time is running out. She plans to tell everyone, but she gets happily stuck in an unexpected snowstorm in her tiny cabin, located outside a small Idaho town.

Deputy Garrett Franke still can't get Trinity out of his mind, especially considering he works side by side with her dad, Sheriff Logan Wilde. When Dawn unexpectedly pulls him aside one day, he allows her to convince him to drive out to a remote cabin in the middle of a snowstorm to check on her sister, whom no one has heard from since the storm hit.

That's the thing about snowstorms: You never know who'll show up at your door, and a baby isn't the kind of secret that can stay that way for long.

Why was it that her phone always rang exactly when the baby went down?

Trinity raced across her cabin in her flannel pajamas and socks. Her cell phone, which she had forgotten to mute, was lit up on the butcher-block counter in the tiny kitchen, ringing like a fire alarm.

"Ah, shit!" she muttered and winced as she stubbed her toe on the leg of a stool she hadn't pushed in. She landed on the phone before it could ring a third time. "Hello?" she whispered, putting all the pissed-off tone she could muster into the word. She stared at the open door to the only bedroom, through which she could just make out the crib. Time stood still as she waited for the cry.

"Whoa, geez, did I wake you?"

It was Dawn, her sister.

Trinity pressed her hand to her chest, over the swell of her breasts, feeling grungy after having opted for sleep instead of a shower. In her pajamas, she felt the chill of the cabin. She needed to get more wood for the fire, too, considering she didn't think it was still going.

"Just got the baby down, and the phone just about woke her," she said. "I was considering a shower even though I'd love nothing more than to grab a few more hours." She groaned and caught a whiff of something off, then lifted her arm and realized it was her. Yup, the shower had now moved up the list of necessities.

"Sleep?" said Dawn. "What the fuck, Trinity? You were supposed to be on the road, remember, for Christmas at Mom and Dad's? You are not going to chicken out! Tell me you're going to show up, please, because if you don't, Mom and Dad are likely to drive up, and then they'll know I've been lying to them. Mom told me just yesterday you were sounding unusually tired, and here's me, having to cover your butt yet again. I said it was likely a deadline, because you've picked up a lot of new clients and are trying to accomplish the impossible, and you were probably pulling an all-nighter again. I swear I can feel my nose grow. I seriously wonder if she can tell I'm lying. Good thing Dad wasn't there, because he'd have known for sure..."

Trinity held the phone away from her ear, still not missing the rest of her sister's rant. Boy, Dawn could get mad when she wanted to, and Trinity knew that the little secret she'd been keeping from everyone except her sister had only dug her into a hole she didn't think she could get out of.

Avoidance was just something she'd become really good at.

"I'm coming," she said. "I told you I would. I was just up most of the night with the baby, and I'm so damn tired I can feel it in my bones. I'm sure you don't want me driving on these roads with a baby, ready to fall asleep." She knew she was spreading it on thick, but at the same time, nervousness had been nipping at her butt again. If she could just find an excuse someone would buy, she'd be able to get out of going home to her parents' place for Christmas. "So stop panicking. I promised I would come and face the music."

Right, the music—which was her parents and the fact that she had a baby only her sister knew about. Like, who did that?

In fact, the baby's father was the real issue: Garrett Franke, her dad's deputy, whom she'd hated since the tenth grade. What had she been thinking? He was tall and dark haired, and she was a sucker for his drawl and smile.

A momentary lapse. She'd not spoken to him once since their night together.

"Look, if you're that tired, I can come and get you," Dawn said. "Even better, how about Mom or Dad—or, better yet, both? Then you can explain about the baby before you see everyone, and I won't have to be there when they realize I've been lying to them for nine months! And while we're at it, Trinity, you need to pick a name for the baby. I gave you my ideas already, so just pick one and go with it."

Dawn's names were all from the list of the top forty in the country—Amelia, Joy, Iris, Kennedy…as if one of them would fit. Trinity strode over to the sink and reached for a glass, then turned on the tap and filled it with water. On the table sat her open laptop and notes from her current client's website design, which was only in the beginning stages. Right, something else she still needed to do. She could finish if only she didn't have to leave her cabin.

There it was again, that wistful longing for a Christmas alone with her baby. Why did the thought appeal to her like the perfect present?

"I told you I'm working on a name," Trinity said. "It

has to be perfect."

"You're kidding, right? She's six weeks old already. Just pick one," Dawn said.

There it was, the constant nagging. Dawn just didn't get the fact that Trinity needed to take her time. She couldn't be pushed. As with learning to swim, she couldn't jump in the deep end of the pool; she needed to wade in carefully to make sure nothing could go wrong.

"Stop pushing, Dawn," she said. "I already told you I'll be there. You don't need to come and get me. I just need to shower and grab some coffee…" And pack up any clean clothes she could find, considering having a new baby meant no laundry was getting done.

She would be driving right into the lion's den, so to speak. She'd avoided Idaho Falls for just that reason. First, Garrett was there, and second, she knew when her parents found out about the baby, they would have a lot of questions she didn't want to answer. Her dad would likely sit her down and start in with his cop interrogation until he found out the real reason she had wanted no one to know.

"So you promise this time you're coming?" Dawn said.

What was it about being put on the spot that made her want to say no?

"Yes, even though I want nothing more than a Christmas alone with my baby without having to sit through Dad's interrogation or Mom's freak-out over the fact that I had a baby and didn't tell them. You said everyone's going to be there, right? All Dad's brothers, and Gram and Gramps and… That's a lot of people, and they're all going to be asking me the one thing I don't want anyone to know: who the father is. You know, maybe Christmas isn't the time for this."

"Don't you dare," Dawn said, and Trinity could feel the bite in her voice. Someone spoke in the background—

she wasn't sure who—before Dawn lowered her voice and said in a loud whisper, "You pack up that baby right now, and figure out a name for her by the time you get here. You get in that four by four and drive, because if you don't, I will tell Mom and Dad…and then there's Garrett."

Trinity didn't miss the threat in her words. "Dawn, don't tell Garrett," she snapped. "You promised me you wouldn't say anything, and I'm holding you to it. I do not want him to know."

"Fine," Dawn replied. "I know what you said, but you can't keep the baby a secret forever. You know that, and I know that. I can't believe I let you talk me into saying nothing. A baby is a really big deal, and the thing about babies is that you can't keep them a secret forever. You know it's not going to take anyone, especially Garrett, too long to figure out from the timeframe that the baby is his. You'd best take the bull by the horns and come clean. He has a right to know, Trinity, no matter what. And then there're Mom and Dad. You know they won't let it go."

She squeezed the phone, furious at her sister, just as she heard the first cry and knew her shower was now going to have to wait. "Fine, but I'm not telling Garrett," she said. "The baby's awake now. I have to go…"

She could hear her sister still talking as she disconnected the phone, furious at the guilt that she didn't want to feel. After all, Garrett was her dad's deputy, and hadn't she heard that he was already hooking up with a friend of Dawn's now?

As she took in her quiet cabin, she wanted nothing more than to have a few more hours of peace and quiet alone with her baby before all hell broke loose and she had to face her mom and dad's inquisition. Worse, she was dreading the minute her dad found out his deputy was in fact the baby's father.

The Holiday Bride,
Chapter 2

"Wow, it's really coming down out there," Dawn said as she dropped into the sheriff's office. "Cars are spinning out of control, and it's practically white-out conditions. Did you get all your Christmas shopping done?"

Something about her was more quirky than usual today. Actually, scratch that. This was the third time Garrett had noticed her coming in, so he took a closer look as she pulled off her gloves and coat and brushed the snow from her short dark hair. Her striking green eyes weren't filled with the usual mischief. Something was off.

"Sure," he replied and lifted his hand to show the Santa mug he was holding, which held stale coffee. It was his gift from the office exchange, from the matronly office manager, Rose. He had drawn the sheriff's name, and he still wasn't sure Logan had appreciated the book of random potty jokes, the first thing he'd seen in the dollar store—though Rose had made it clear that ten dollars was the limit and they would have to be creative. "You looking for your dad? Because he's out on a call and asked me to hold down the office. Not sure how long he'll be, Dawn."

She just made a face and shrugged. "No, I'm not here to see my dad. Thought I'd stop in and bug you, is all."

This was odd. He couldn't help thinking she was up to something. "In the middle of a snowstorm?" he said, doing his best not to laugh. As she leaned against his desk, he could see she didn't appreciate being called out. There was just something about her today that went beyond the usual Dawn weirdness.

The fax dinged and started spitting out paper, and he found himself taking in the way Dawn lingered as he walked over to it. Was she flirting? No, but she definitely wanted something. He said nothing.

"So what are you and Lori doing for Christmas, again?" she said.

He reached for the papers, seeing the notes from the sheriff a county over, an arrest report and a summary of road conditions. The unexpected storm wasn't really unexpected, considering snow and white-out conditions were the norm every winter. He was prepared for a long Christmas of calls, likely all of them vehicle-related, because it seemed everyone forgot how to drive as soon as the first snowflake fell.

He tossed Dawn a sideways glance. Something about her smile seemed off, something he couldn't put his finger on. She was up to something. Maybe.

"Nothing," he replied. "I'm working over Christmas. Your dad needs someone to man the phones and the office, and that's me. I drew the short straw. That's the single life."

He and Lori were on the back burner, taking a break, considering she had suddenly wanted to change their casual relationship into a commitment, and that kind of said everything about where their relationship was going.

At the same time, he wasn't about to share anything from his personal life with Dawn, considering it would likely all go right to his boss, her dad.

He'd already made the mistake of mixing business with pleasure once—with Trinity.

"Hmm," was all she said, and he took another second to look down at her. She was cute, attractive, slim, and the spitting image of her sister. He had to look away.

"So what's going on, Dawn? You want something?" he said as he walked the papers over to Rose's empty desk. Seeing nothing urgent, he rested them in her inbox for her to deal with.

"Just wanted to talk to you and catch up, is all," she said. "We haven't done that in quite a while. I only see you when I drop in to see Dad or when you're out on patrol or something. I kind of miss that lopsided smile and all that handsomeness."

He dragged his gaze back over to her, and she flashed him another one of her cute smiles. She was wearing blue jeans, and her hiking boots were caked in snow.

"You hitting on me there, Dawn?"

The shock in her expression was priceless. "What? No!" She actually reached out and swatted his arm, and he was at least glad he had settled that issue. He blew out a breath of relief. "You think I want to be added to the list of ladies you can't or won't commit to? Seriously, Garrett, you may be a hot, confident, arrogant cop, and those pretty-boy features of yours may have all the women you date thinking that they can get their hooks into you and find a way to settle you down, but I'm not one of them. Besides, aren't you and Lori still an item?" She lifted her hands, and he took her in. She could be amusing at times, but something about the way she had said it and the way she kept prying had him trying to figure out what was really up with her.

"Lori and I aren't serious," he said. "Everyone knows that. So if this isn't you hitting on me, then what gives, Dawn? And aren't you dating that rich dude again, Dwayne Do-gooder or whatever the hell his name is?"

She was unimpressed. Then again, he recalled that her dad, the sheriff, had even asked him to run a background check on the guy. "You know his name is Hadley Reynolds," Dawn said, "and we're kind of taking a break." She shrugged and slapped her gloves together, and he wasn't sure what to make of her expression. "He's in Germany right now, handling some crisis, and we decided to cool things down. Considering he hops on a plane every time some disaster happens, it makes it kind of difficult to build a relationship. More often than not, we're in opposite time zones. When I call him, he's asleep, and then he calls me back and it's the middle of the night."

She forced one of those uncomfortable smiles to her face again, and this time he really looked at the way she was standing, her expression. Her casual dismissal didn't seem all that convincing, and she was now gripping the cell phone she had pulled from her coat pocket, the second time she'd looked at it.

"Okay, spill," Garrett said. "Something's up, and I hardly think you're here just to chat. What's really going on? And no more bullshit." He tacked the snow report and notice of a road closure on the interstate up on the bulletin board and walked back over to his desk.

Dawn squeezed her phone and then lifted her hands. "Fine. Look, Trinity was supposed to be on her way. She's coming home for Christmas and should be here by now, but I haven't heard from her. I've been calling her cell phone, and now it says she can't be reached, which likely means the cell towers are down. If I didn't make it clear, the snow is really coming down…" She bit her lip, and he had a sinking feeling he wasn't going to like this.

He said nothing as he stared down at her. Yeah, Trinity and him were like oil and water, not something he wanted to talk about. Nor did he want to relive their one night together, which never should have happened. What about sleeping with his boss's daughter had he thought was a good idea at the time? All her sass and back talk, her smart mouth… He pulled in a breath and forced her sweet, sexy image from his mind once again. *Nope, not going to happen!*

"And why aren't you talking to your dad about this?" Garrett said. "Just FYI, she probably took a look at the snow and realized the smart thing to do was stay put. At least one of you two has some sense."

Dawn grabbed his arm, her entire demeanor switching from playful to desperate. "Look, Garrett, seriously, as you said, my dad is out on a call. I'm worried. I mean, I could go looking for her, but the road conditions are questionable, and if I head up the mountain where she insisted on buying that damn cabin, I'll likely end up in a ditch, and then my dad will wonder where I am, considering I promised my mom I'd help her with baking and getting the house ready for the holidays…"

He knew his mouth was open. He lifted his gaze to the ceiling as she went on and on, knowing Logan would be furious that Garrett had suggested Dawn handle this when he should go himself. At the same time, why wasn't his boss already all over this? After all, Trinity was his daughter.

"Stop!" Garrett snapped. "Give me your sister's number, and I'll call her. If she doesn't answer, then I'll go up there and see that she's fine. At least she had enough sense to stay put."

Dawn squealed and threw her arms around him,

reaching up over his shoulders and bouncing up and down. Then she jumped back, her expression suddenly excited—no, overjoyed. Of course, he couldn't help but smile.

"That's great," she said. "I'll write down her number for you, but then you hop right into your truck and drive up to where she lives." She reached for a pen and paper on his desk and gestured to him. "Oh, and don't take no for an answer from her if she's there. Just pack her up and bring her here. Don't leave her in the cabin, because it's Christmas, and she promised everyone she'd be here."

He just stared down at Dawn as she scribbled out Trinity's phone number and address. He couldn't help thinking this was what she'd planned before walking through the door. What was it with women? Either they were trying to get a ring on his finger, or they were trying to work some angle and make him think it was his idea.

It was no wonder he was still single—and happily so. Yeah, he definitely had no plans to get tied up in that trap at any time in the foreseeable future.

Dawn lifted her hand in a wave as she skipped out of the office, and Garrett just shook his head and folded up the paper.

"Women," he muttered under his breath.

"Lorhainne Eckhart is one of my go to authors when I want a guaranteed good book. So many twists and turns, but also so much love and such a strong sense of family."

(LORA W., REVIEWER)

New York Times & USA Today bestseller Lorhainne Eckhart is best known for writing Raw Relatable Real Romance where "Morals and family are running themes." As one fan calls her, she is the "Queen of the family saga." (aherman) writing "the ups and downs of what goes on within a family but also with some suspense, angst and of course a bit of romance thrown in for good measure."

Follow Lorhainne on Bookbub to receive alerts on New Releases and Sales and join her mailing list at Lorhainne-Eckhart.com for her Monday Blog, all book news, give-aways and FREE reads. With over 120 books, audiobooks, and multiple series published and available at all, retailers now translated into six languages. She is a multiple recipient of the Readers' Favorite Award for Suspense and Romance, and lives in the Pacific Northwest on an island, is the mother of three, her oldest has autism and she is an advocate for never giving up on your dreams.

"Lorhainne Eckhart has this uncanny way of just hitting the spot every time with her books."

(CAROLINE L., REVIEWER)

The O'Connells: *The O'Connells of Livingston, Montana are not your typical family. A riveting collection of stories surrounding the ups and downs of what goes on within a family but also with some suspense, angst and of course a bit of romance thrown in for good measure. "I thought I loved the Friessens, but I absolutely adore the O'Con-nell's. Each and every book has different genres of stories, but the one thing in common is how she is able to wrap it around the family, which is the heart of each story." (C. Logue)*

The Friessens: *An emotional big family romance series, the Friessen family siblings find their relationships tested, lay their hearts on the line, and discover lasting love! "Lorhainne Eckhart is one of my go to authors when I want* *a guaranteed good book. So many twists and turns, but also so much love and such a strong sense of family." (Lora W., Reviewer)*

The Parker Sisters: *The Parker Sisters are a close-knit family, and like any other family they have their ups and downs. Eckhart has crafted another intense family drama… "The character development is outstanding, and the emotional investment is high…" (Aherman, Reviewer)*

The McCabe Brothers: *Join the five McCabe siblings on their journeys to the dark and dangerous side of love! An intense, exhilarating collection of romantic thrillers you won't want to miss. — "Eckhart has a new series that is definitely worth the read. The queen of the family saga started this series with a spin-off of her wildly successful Friessen series." From a Readers' Favorite award—winning author and "queen of the family saga" (Aherman)*

Billy Jo McCabe Mystery: *The social worker and the cop, an unlikely couple drawn together on a small, secluded Pacific Northwest island where nothing is as it seems. Protecting the innocent comes at a cost, and what seems to be a sleepy, quiet town is anything but.*

Lorhainne loves to hear from her readers! You can connect with me at:
www.LorhainneEckhart.com
lorhainneeckhart.le@gmail.com

In the Charm
Unexpected Consequences
It Was Always You
The First Time I Saw You
Welcome to My Arms
Welcome to Boston
I'll Always Love You
Ground Rules
A Reason to Breathe
You Are My Everything
Anything For You
The Homecoming
Stay Away From My Daughter
The Bad Boy
A Place of Our Own
The Visitor
All About Devon
Long Past Dawn
How to Heal a Heart
Keep Me In Your Heart

The O'Connells
The Neighbor
The Third Call
The Secret Husband
The Quiet Day
The Commitment
The Missing Father
The Hometown Hero
Justice
The Family Secret
The Fallen O'Connell
The Return of the O'Connells
And The She Was Gone

The Stalker
The O'Connell Family Christmas
The Girl Next Door
Broken Promises
The Gatekeeper
The Hunted

The McCabe Brothers
Don't Stop Me
Don't Catch Me
Don't Run From Me
Don't Hide From Me
Don't Leave Me
Out of Time

A Billy Jo McCabe Mystery
Nothing As it Seems
Hiding in Plain Sight
The Cold Case
The Trap
Above the Law
The Stranger at the Door
The Children
The Last Stand
The Charity
The Sacrifice

The Street Fighter
Finding Home

The Wilde Brothers
The One
The Honeymoon, A Wilde Brothers Short
Friendly Fire

Not Quite Married, A Wilde Brothers Short
A Matter of Trust
The Reckoning, A Wilde Brothers Christmas
Traded
Unforgiven
The Holiday Bride

Married in Montana
His Promise
Love's Promise
A Promise of Forever

The Parker Sisters
Thrill of the Chase
The Dating Game
Play Hard to Get
What We Can't Have
Go Your Own Way
A June Wedding

Kate & Walker
One Night
Edge of Night
Last Night

Walk the Right Road Series
The Choice
Lost and Found
Merkaba
Bounty
Blown Away: The Final Chapter
He Came Back

The Saved Series

Saved
Vanished
Captured

Single Titles
Loving Christine